DROWNED
AT
DAWN

(Tracy Sterling Book 3)

By RJ Law

DROWNED AT DAWN
(Tracy Sterling Book 3)

Chapter 1

Caroline stumbled through the swampy woods, her heart racing as she fled through the inky-black night. All around her, bullfrogs croaked and crickets chirped. Somewhere in the distance, men laughed as the beams of their flashlights danced in the darkness.

As one of the lights swept over the space before her, she paused a moment, her heart thundering within her chest. And then, when it moved on, she ran, each step a squelch against the damp soil as she burrowed deeper and deeper into the humid, insect-fogged night.

Soon, the trail turned into no trail at all, and she held her arms out like a blind woman, searching her way amid the stinging lashes of whipping tree branches. The swampland air was a damp shroud clinging to her skin, hot and heavy and tinged with the odor of soil and decay.

Her heart pounded as she sucked in frantic breaths, the scent of brackish water and decaying leaves filling her senses, each gulping breath followed by an involuntary gag.

She slowed for a moment to catch her breath, her chest afire as she bent and propped her hands against her dirty knees. She breathed and breathed the sickening air.

More laughter. Closer this time.

A crunch echoed in the night only a few yards away.

Frantically, Caroline began to move, her shoes sinking into the swampy undergrowth as she bolted through the dense vegetation. As she ran, vines snagged at her clothes and branches whipped at her face, leaving thin lines of red against her sweating skin.

And still, she ran, her tired legs moving of their own volition, propelling her through the marsh. But soon, a deep fatigue stripped away her vigor, and she slowed to a stumble before tripping on a thick tree root. Flailing wildly, she felt her face slam against the soggy earth, and despite her best efforts, a little groan escaped her mouth.

"Over here!" called a deep male voice.

Bone-weary, Caroline groped around, her hands sliding over slimy vegetation, seeking a broken branch, a rock, any form of defense. But all she felt was the wriggle of oversized insects. So, she yanked her hand away and staggered to her feet.

Now, the footfalls grew louder, closer, until they were almost upon her.

Out of the darkness, a hand, harsh and unyielding, surged toward her and closed around her arm. She cried out, yanking free, and instinctively swung, her elbow connecting with a solid form. A raspy groan of pain detonated in the shadows, and she was free.

Invigorated by fear, Caroline ran, her feet sliding over the marshy terrain, each squelching step echoing the beat of her heart. She could hear her pursuers behind her, their curses muffled by the marsh's symphony of nocturnal life.

Soon, she was swallowed up by the twisted cypress trees, their gnarled roots like skeletal hands reaching from the marshy ground. The voices grew fainter in her wake, as she fled blindly into the swamp, the woods greedily embracing her with their thorny, unforgiving arms.

Now, her breath came in ragged gasps, the humid air making each inhalation a fight. Suddenly, her foot struck something hard, sending her sprawling onto an old, warped dock that stretched out toward a murky pond.

In the stark moonlight, the water lay ahead, a stagnant pool dotted with rotting lily pads. Underneath the dock, things stared back, their eyes aglow in the refracted moonlight, unseen water creatures lurking in the shadowy depths.

She gasped as she tried to catch her breath, the sharp tang of damp earth and putrid water filling her senses, the air thick with the rancid scent of wet, warm decay.

The old wood groaned as she scrambled to her feet, glancing back just as the beam of a flashlight cut through the darkness. Without thinking, she ran, each thud of her heart matched by the drumming of her shoes on the old wooden planks.

As the flashlight grew brighter behind her, she stumbled forward out over the old, warped dock, its end lost to the darkness where it stretched out over the still, black pond. The wood groaned as she moved over the weather-beaten boards, some live thing splashing in the waters in response to the disturbance.

Her heart pounded in her ears, a thunderous tempo matching the harsh rhythm of the heavy boot steps closing in behind her. As she neared the end of the dock, she searched for a path of escape, her mind spinning in a whirl of desperation.

But there was nothing. Only the dark expanse of the stagnant waters, where the moon cast its pallid glow over the stinking black-mirror surface, as the horizon began to color with the coming dawn.

Her panic rose like the tide, choking her, drowning her in its depths.

Behind her, the footsteps grew louder, and the dock gave a final, agonizing creak. And then, a scream split the dying night, as heavy arms closed around her. And creatures splashed in the low waters as the dock gave a few final jerks, before everything grew still again, and silence fell upon the swamp.

Chapter 2

Tracy sat in the waiting room at the little law office. To her right, a little old woman sat at a small reception desk, her eyes peering over a pair of designer glasses as she pecked away at a keyboard. Tick, tick, tick, went her fingers, as the air conditioner hummed amid a steady stream of classical music playing from speakers overhead.

In the seat to Tracy's right, a very large woman read a magazine, her double chin concealed by a big bulging neck brace that stretched her chin upward, so she had to cast her eyes downward to view the printed text.

The old woman coughed, while the clock on the wall above the reception desk kept time. Tracy took a breath and tapped her foot. Across the room, on one far wall, there was a framed photo centered prominently for all to see. In it, the lawyer shook hands with a celebrity Tracy couldn't place, a big grin on his face as he posed for the camera. She looked at it and shook her head. Then, she straightened in her seat and yawned, while the clicks of the woman's typing filled the air.

"Ms. Sterling," said the receptionist at last.

Tracy looked over at the woman.

"He'll see you now."

Tracy stood up and stretched her back. She glanced at the injured woman, who tilted her body to look up. Then, she turned and made her way toward the lawyer's office.

"Hello," he said as she opened the door. "Come on in."

Tracy entered and shut the door behind her. The office was decorated with pictures of the smiling attorney. On one side of the room, there was a little beige sofa with floral designs. On the other, there was a liquor cabinet with a small bar. The lawyer himself sat behind a very expensive-looking hardwood desk, which contrasted with his ordinary-looking suit. In his late thirties, he had dark brown hair that had begun to recede. He wasn't ugly, nor was he handsome. He was ordinary-looking, just like the rest of the room.

"My name's Howard," he said as he stood and offered his hand.

She approached and gave it a shake.

"Tracy Sterling."

He nodded.

"Please have a seat."

They both sat, and he smiled.

"I got your name from a mutual acquaintance."

"Oh?" she said. "Who might that be?"

"Jimmy Hunter."

Tracy frowned.

"And how do you know Jimmy?" she asked.

Howard shrugged.

"I'm a lawyer. He has needed my service from time to time."

Tracy nodded.

"I'll bet."

Howard shook his head.

"No, it's not like that." He paused for a moment. "Or I guess sometimes it is. Jimmy's Jimmy, after all."

She nodded.

"He certainly is."

"Anyway," said Howard. "He and I go way back. And he says you're one of the best."

Tracy raised her eyebrows.

"He said that?"

Howard nodded.

"Yes. Was he mistaken?"

She shrugged.

"It's all relative, I suppose. Can you tell me what this is about?"

"Sure," he said. "I might have a job for you."

She nodded.

"What kind of job?"

He sat back in his chair, a nice leather piece that was far too fine a thing for the rest of the office.

"I've been hired by a local woman," he said. "Her nephew has been arrested for murder. I need a good PI to dig into his background and help investigate his side of the story."

She nodded.

"What's the pay?"

He smiled.

"20 grand upfront. Another 20 when you're done."

She raised her eyebrows.

"Why so much? What's the catch?"

He furrowed his brows a little.

"Well, the catch is that the case isn't here. It's in South Carolina."

She furrowed her brows.

"South Carolina?"

He nodded.

"The client is originally from there. She moved to New York in her twenties. But she still has a sister who lives in South Carolina. The sister doesn't have the money for a local attorney. So, the client wants to help. And she doesn't have a high opinion of the local offerings, I guess you could say. So, she hired me, and here we are."

Tracy frowned.

"So, I go with you to South Carolina and see if I can find some details to help you create a defense?"

He nodded.

"That's right. Or, ideally, you help me dig up some details that will compel the district attorney to drop the case. Either way, you'll earn full commission no matter what."

She thought for a moment as she considered his offer. There was a ring from a coffee cup on the desk, and she scratched at it absent-mindedly.

"Why me?" she asked. "Why not just give the job to Jimmy?"

"Well, Jimmy's not really an option. Not for this particular case."

"Why not?"

Howard shrugged.

"Well, let's just say this case might require a little more finesse. Anyway, he wouldn't take the case if I offered it to him."

She raised her eyebrows.

"And why not?"

"Because," he said. "Jimmy's afraid of flying."

Tracy sat back in her chair as a smile leaked from the corner of her mouth.

"Are you serious?"

He nodded.

"Terrified."

Tracy shook her head, and they both shared a smile.

"Oh, Jimmy," Tracy said.

Howard raised his brows.

"Well, I think it might be the only thing he's afraid of. But he won't do it under any circumstances. So, he gave me your name and number. And here we are."

Tracy nodded.

"So, we fly down to South Carolina, and I try to dig up some details on your client?"

"That's right," he said. "I'll put you up in a hotel. Cover your expenses. You talk to some people. Do your thing. See if you can help me prove his innocence. Or his guilt. If he's guilty, I'll see if I can get him a plea agreement. If not, I'll try to put together a defense. Either way, I'll probably cut you loose pretty quickly, and you can fly home with a pretty decent payday."

Tracy shrugged.

"Well," she said. "I can give you a couple of weeks, I suppose."

He nodded.

"That's probably all I will need. But I'm flying out Tuesday morning. And I'd like to have you with me if possible."

She started to stand.

"That shouldn't be a problem."

He stood up and held out a hand.

"Excellent," he said as they shook.

He sat back down as she turned for the door.

"Don't you want to know who the client is accused of killing?" Howard asked as she walked away.

She paused and turned.

"Just fill me in on the plane," she said. "The more I know, the more likely I am to change my mind."

He raised his eyebrows and nodded.

"Fair enough."

The next couple of days passed too quickly, and Tracy spent the time frantically tying up several loose ends. A client owed her some money. And she wasted an afternoon tracking him down at a local pub, where he spewed a fountain of excuses as she pinned him to the barstool with an icy glare. Even then, he only paid her a quarter of what he owed her after claiming his assets had been frozen by his faithless wife. In effect, he said, Tracy had been too good at her job, proving the wife's infidelity well enough to spark a contentious divorce.

A day later, the irony still filled her thoughts as she drove to the airport to meet Howard and fly to South Carolina to do what exactly? She wasn't entirely sure. And now the whole thing seemed like a foolish excursion from a life that needed a fresh appraisal. Or, at minimum, maybe a date. She shook these thoughts away and took the exit to the airport.

After stowing her vehicle in the parking garage and making her way through security, she found the lawyer waiting at the boarding gate, a friendly smile on his face as he gestured to the seat next to him.

"You made it," he said.

She plopped down and dropped her bag next to her.

"Sorry I'm late. I had to check my gun with baggage security."

He frowned at this and sat quietly until they boarded the plane. The silence continued, while the flight attendants gave their safety speech, robotic arms moving about as they stared ahead with glassy eyes. Then, the plane started moving, and Howard broke the silence.

"Do you really think you'll need a weapon?" he asked.

She looked at him.

"You never know. Anyway, I don't ever work without one."

He nodded.

"I understand," he said as the plane rode the wind upward. "It's just that I'm not looking to stir up trouble. I just want you to gather some facts. Preferably as delicately as possible."

Tracy shrugged.

"Sometimes, when you start gathering facts, people get nervous. And nervous people are liable to do anything to protect themselves if you start uncovering the wrong details. Anyway, don't worry. I'm not planning to cause any trouble."

He nodded.

"Fair enough."

As the plane leveled off amid a cloudless sky, the passenger in front of Tracy pushed her seat back. Tracy flexed her jaw as the hard plastic back clanked against her knees. Howard yawned and looked out the window, where the city turned toy-like beneath their god-like eyes.

"Well," said Tracy. "It's a two-hour flight. Why don't you start filling me on the case?"

Howard looked at her and scratched his jaw.

"I don't really know a whole lot," he said. "Not yet, at least. Just what the aunt told me. As I understand it, her sister's son—Peter is his name—is accused of killing his girlfriend. They were visiting her hometown, some little community out in the boondocks. Anyway, while they were there, she was killed apparently, and the local sheriff immediately arrested him."

Tracy glared at the woman sitting in front of her and shifted her knees.

"How was she killed?"

"Drowned," said Howard. "Or at least that's what the local forensics people said. Mind you, these are probably just local physicians at a little podunk hospital."

Tracy frowned.

"Were there drugs in her system?"

Howard shook his head.

"No drugs, no alcohol."

She thought for a moment.

"So, there was no murder weapon. Why arrest the boyfriend? Did someone see him in the act?"

Howard shook his head.

"I don't think anyone saw anything. She was found in a pond out deep in the woods. As I understand it, this is some really thick country. Swamps and such. Like the kind with alligators. These people who live out in that shit, they're different. Or at least that's how the aunt described it when she hired me. Anyway, we'll know more when we talk to the boyfriend."

Tracy looked at him.

"When will that be?"

"Today," he said. "I've already set up a visit at the Charleston jail. We'll rent a car and head over there after we land."

A couple of hours later, the plane landed in Charleston. Tracy and Howard got to their feet and flowed out with other passengers into the airport terminal. They waited half an hour for baggage to deliver

11

Tracy's pistol, which was locked up tight in a black steel case. When they had their things, they stepped outside into the hot, humid South Carolina air, and Tracy immediately felt her shirt stick to her sweating back.

"Jesus," she said as she looked up at the sky.

A small, stifling sun hung in the flawless blue heavens, its relentless glare cooking the pavement below their feet.

"Yeah," said Howard as he stripped off his sport coat.

They made their way to the car rental facility, and Howard rented a modest vehicle, its primary attribute a fully functioning air conditioner, which Tracy dialed to the max.

It was another half-hour before they arrived at the jailhouse. Rising above the skyline from a distance, the imposing structure sat upon the landscape like a great concrete fortress. Tracy leaned down to eye the prison as they pulled into the lot.

The bright Charleston sun held dominion over the great stone building. Relentlessly oppressive, its bright light cast a stark contrast between the detention center's grim shadows and high sun-bleached walls, which sheltered some of the state's most violent criminals.

There were murderers. There were rapists. And there was Peter Teller, who claimed to be neither, at least according to his aunt. Tracy didn't really know whether he was neither or both. And already, she was having trouble adopting Howard's view that his client was completely innocent if for no other reason than because his aunt had paid the lawyer's asking price.

She assessed the looming structure as they both stepped out of the rental car. A humid breeze whispered through the sparse, heat-stricken vegetation framing the entrance. A solitary bird circled high overhead, its figure small amid the sweltering cloudless sky.

Howard looked at her and followed her gaze to the bird. Then, he looked at the building, and they headed toward the entrance. Inside, they were embraced by a cool, sterile gush of conditioned air. Without speaking, they walked across the polished linoleum floor, the rhythmic clip-clop of their shoes echoing through the austere corridors.

Their arrival had been expected, and after waiting a few minutes, a prison officer in a starched uniform approached, his keychain jangling with every step. They stood up from a pair of stiff plastic chairs and followed him through a labyrinth of stark corridors, each one lit by harsh fluorescent lights. Their brief journey was quiet, save for the intermittent sounds of shouting men and the occasional clank of security doors.

Finally, they were led into a stark room, one of many consultation areas in the facility. Inside, there was nothing more than a heavy steel table and a few mismatched chairs. The officer showed them in and left without a word. Tracy watched him go and then turned to look at Howard, who shrugged and set his briefcase on the table.

She looked around and sniffed the air. The room held a lingering scent of antiseptic, cigarettes, stale coffee and recycled air. One wall had the tiniest rectangular window, the outside world reduced to a sliver of blue sky and a parking lot glutted with cars.

She looked at Howard, who was busy flipping through some notes he'd written on a yellow legal pad. The hum of the overhead lights filled the silence as they waited, their shadows pooling around their feet, which tapped involuntarily as they awaited Peter Teller.

Minutes passed in this sterile bubble, the world outside seemingly held at bay. And then, the door opened once more. Framed by the harsh light of the corridor, a sad figure of a young man shuffled into the room, his posture bent, ankles hobbled together by a heavy leg iron chain. He had a black eye, and his face was swollen on one side. Other than that, he looked soft and young, and his plain blue eyes sheltered the makings of a river that he somehow held at bay, even as his chin trembled like something that had been electrified.

Tracy and Howard both stood as he entered. Howard looked at the guard.

"What happened to him?"

The guard looked impassive.

"Must have looked at somebody wrong."

Tracy pointed at the leg irons.

"Are those really necessary?"

The guard shrugged without speaking.

"You've got an hour," he said.

He turned and left the room, closing the door behind him. When he was gone, Peter shuffled to one of the chairs and sat, his face showing obvious exhaustion. There was a pitcher of murky water on the table, and Howard poured the boy a glass.

"Here," he said as he slid it over. "Drink this."

Without speaking, Peter took the glass with a trembling hand. He took a few sips and set it down. They watched while he ran a sleeve across his mouth.

"Did my mom send you?"

Howard nodded.

"Your aunt," he said. "My name is Howard. I'll be representing you. This is Tracy. She's an investigator who will be assisting me."

Peter blinked up at them, one of his eyes squinting into the fluorescent light, the other completely swollen shut.

"They said no bail," he said.

Howard nodded.

"Yes, I'm afraid you're being held without bail. You will have to stay here until the trial. Or until we can find information that might compel the district attorney to drop the charges."

Peter took in a great shuddering breath.

"What kind of information?"

Howard sat down in a chair.

"Well, let's just start by telling us what happened."

Peter shook his head.

"I don't know what happened," he said. "All I know is they said Caroline drowned. And they think I had something to do with it."

Tracy frowned at him as she took a seat.

"Let's just start from the beginning," she said. "Tell us how you and Caroline met. How you ended up in Reedsville in the first place."

He gave a little nod and took in a deep breath.

"We met in college here in Charleston. We'd been dating a few months." He sighed and shook his head as he stared down at the table. "She told me she was from a small town out in the low country. Out with the alligators and all the backwood hicks."

He took in another faltering breath and sighed.

"She had this adorable accent. So, it wasn't hard to imagine. But she was smart too. Real smart. Smarter than me. And she hated that place. She told me she was the first in her family to get out and go to college and that she never wanted to go back."

Howard wrote on his legal pad.

"Why did she go back?" he asked.

Peter swallowed.

"Her mom got sick," he said. "So, she felt like she had to go back to visit. And I offered to go with her. But she wouldn't have it. I think she was ashamed. She didn't want me to see where she'd come

14

from. Or at least that's what it seemed like. Anyway, I insisted. And after a while, she gave in. And we drove down together."

"And what happened when you got there?" Tracy asked.

He shook his head at the table.

"I immediately regretted it. Reedsville is fucked up. And I don't just mean in the small backwards town kind of way. There's something weird about that place. I could immediately see why she never wanted to go back."

Howard stopped writing and set his pen down.

"Weird, like how?"

Peter shook his head.

"I don't know. It's the way people are, I guess. The way they look at you. It's like they all know each other. And they can tell you're from somewhere else the moment they lay eyes on you. And they don't like it. Not one bit. And they aren't afraid to tell you how they feel about things. About you being in their town. About the world you came from. They sneer at you on the street. They eye you from across a bar. They whisper about you. I know it sounds strange, but it's kind of chilling. At least it was for me."

Tracy nodded.

"Did anyone give you trouble while you were there? Someone who might have had reason to harm Caroline?"

Peter nodded.

"Oh, yes," he said. "A group of guys she went to high school with. I don't know their names. But they were on us the moment we got into town. They harassed us in a local bar. They harassed us out on a dirt road. Tailgating us. Honking horns. It was a nightmare."

Tracy and Howard exchanged looks.

"And these boys, you don't know their names?"

Peter shook his head.

"No, but it shouldn't be that hard to figure out. That town is small. And they roam around the place like they own it. I think they're important. Or their parents are anyway."

Howard nodded.

"What happened on the night of Caroline's murder?"

Peter sniffed a little and swallowed hard.

"I'm sorry," he said with a catch in his throat. "It still doesn't seem real."

Tracy watched him with a hard stare, while Howard gave him a comforting smile.

15

"It's ok," he said. "Take your time."

Peter rubbed his eyes and swallowed again.

"We were staying in a little hotel room because her mom's house was just too cramped. And her brother lived there too, so there was just no room. We'd been there three days, and it was our last night, and Caroline said she was going to drive out to her mom's place and say goodbye. So, I stayed behind in the hotel room. After a few hours, when it got dark, and she still wasn't back, I called her mom. And she said Caroline never showed up. So, I got scared and called the local sheriff. And then, the next morning, he showed up at my room and arrested me. No explanation. They just said Caroline was dead, and I was under arrest."

Howard and Tracy frowned at each other.

"Why do you think the police fingered you so quickly?" asked Tracy.

Peter shook his head.

"I have no idea. I never left the hotel room that night. Not one time. But they say there are witnesses that saw me leave. But if there are, they're lying. Because I just laid in bed watching TV the whole time."

Howard jotted something onto his legal pad.

"Alright, Peter," he said. "Is there anything you're leaving out? Anything that might incriminate you? I need to know now, so we don't get blindsided down the road."

Peter shook his head.

"No way," he said. "Me and Caroline barely ever fought. And I wouldn't hurt anyone for any reason. This is some bullshit backwoods coverup. The police there are corrupt. They're trying to pin this on me because I'm not from there. Or they're trying to cover for someone."

Howard looked at Tracy, who was drumming her fingers on the table.

"Ok," she said. "I'll go down there and see what I can learn."

Peter's eyes flicked up.

"You're going to Reedsville?"

Tracy nodded.

"How else am I going to learn something?"

The boy sniffed.

"You're not going to like it."

Tracy shrugged.

"I'm from New York. I've seen my share of fucked up shit."

16

He shook his head.

"Not like this."

She gave him a doubtful look and then sat quietly while Howard finished the interview. An hour later, they stepped out of the prison and back into the suffocating heat. High above, the bird still circled, like a scavenger waiting for some limping beast to finally die.

"I need to borrow the car," said Tracy.

Howard looked at her.

"Why don't I just go with you?"

Tracy looked at him.

"No," she said. "I can't show up with a lawyer. No one will talk to me. I need a cover."

He looked her up and down.

"I don't think you're going to blend in down there."

She gave him a closed-lip smile.

"I'll think of something."

He rubbed his jaw thoughtfully.

"Well," he said. "I'll give you a couple of days. And then I'll find my way down there. I need to get a look at this place myself."

She nodded.

"I'll drop you off at your hotel."

An hour later, Tracy drove alone down a long stretch of road that cut a winding path through some of the thickest forest she had ever seen. In no time at all, the regimented order of civilization faded into the distance, and the landscape shifted, morphing into a riot of verdant hues. Imposing cypress trees loomed over the road, their knotted roots submerged in the marshy terrain. Ferns and reeds added vibrant brushstrokes to the tableau, while tufts of wildflowers burst out in colorful bunches amid all the crowded green.

As she rounded tight corners, the landscape unfurled outside the window, a spectacle of vegetative overgrowth against the backdrop of a clear summer sky. The intricate grid of New York's streets and alleyways, the familiar high-rises, and the ceaseless clamor were nowhere to be seen. Instead, an alien canvas lay before her, draped in lush greenery and threaded with marshes that spilled into the land like some vivid watercolor dream. All around, the air seemed to bristle with life, birds picking at roadkill carcasses in the road, insects splatting into grotesque splotches of abstract art against her windshield.

Here and there, small, decrepit shacks peaked from within the mossy shroud of thicket, their boards rotting away down into the rich loam, laden with the weight of generations past.

As she ventured deeper into the foreign landscape, the scenery grew progressively intricate. Wildlife appeared more frequently, darting forms visible in brief flashes before they disappeared back into the underbrush. With every rounded bend in the road, heavy, humid air rushed in from her open windows, the scent of damp earth, foul bog water and the faintly sweet aroma of blooming jasmine wafting in.

After another hour, the surroundings changed again, the scenery evolving into a haunting landscape that loomed eerily along the edges of the road. Spanish moss hung from the trees like ghostly drapes, the wet soil changed from clay red to black loam, semi-submerged alligators drifting lazily in a swamp, their eyes glinting like sharp jewels beneath the veil of muddy water.

Deeper still, Tracy ventured into the realm of marshes and moss, her city-bred driving skills tested by the narrow lanes that dissected the endless wilderness. And then, out of nowhere, the lights of a small town finally began to twinkle into existence.

To her right, a small sign said, 'Welcome to Reedsville,' it's metal pockmarked with bullet holes from a low-caliber rifle. In the other lane, a truck barreled away from the town, the bearded driver slowing to eye her with furrowed curiosity as the two vehicles passed.

Soon, Tracy breached the forest walls and emerged amid the little circle of civilization, its humble buildings clustered together under the vast Southern sky. As she drove into the town, the trees retreated, replaced by houses, gas stations, and the occasional church, their sharp, white steeples jutting into the late afternoon sky.

Tracy entered the town and followed the main road into an abbreviated downtown area. She slowed and parked amid a row of old pickup trucks. Along the sidewalk, people passed, their eyes flicking toward her as she stepped out of her vehicle.

The street was lined with several short brick buildings that housed an assortment of small businesses. A pharmacy, a feed store, a little bar with neon beer signs in the window.

Tracy shut her door and entered the pharmacy. Inside, an old man sat at the counter counting pills. Tracy approached and started to speak. The man held up a finger without looking at her, his lips moving as he passed pills from one small pile to another.

Tracy stood and waited while a thickly set middle-aged woman got in line behind her.

At last, the old pharmacist finished and looked up at Tracy. He stood upon a platform behind a big wooden counter, his high perch giving him an air of authority, like a judge overseeing the conduct of lesser men.

"Yes?" he said with a thick Southern accent.

"Hello," said Tracy. "Can you tell me where the local hotel is?"

The man looked at her thoughtfully as he sucked one side of his cheek.

"You visitin someone?"

"Not exactly," said Tracy.

The man looked past Tracy toward the woman in line behind her, and the two seemed to share a thought. He frowned down at Tracy, his old, weathered face wrinkling as he took several breaths.

"Well," said the man at last. "There's the Blue Bonnet down the street. There's also some cabins a little further down if that's what you prefer."

Tracy gave a polite smile.

"Thank you."

The man wrinkled up his forehead and looked her over.

"Whereabouts are you from?"

Tracy raised her eyebrows.

"All over, really."

The old man's frown deepened.

"That so?"

Tracy nodded.

"Thanks again," she said as she turned away.

"Yep," said the man as he and the woman watched her leave the store.

Outside, the setting sun cast long shadows over the streets. Tracy hurried to her car and made her way down the main road until she saw a sign that said Blue Bonnet Hotel.

The weathered two-story structure was painted in a faded robin's egg blue that had begun to chip and peel. An old sodden deck seemed to give a little as Tracy crossed it and entered the building.

Inside, there was a small, dimly lit reception area. It had an old, slightly sweet aroma that reminded Tracy of her grandmother's attic. The walls were decorated with flowery wallpaper that was beginning to lose its color. And the reception counter held a small bell, its brass surface polished to perfection.

"Evening, dear," came a soft, drawling voice.

The woman behind the counter was of advanced years, her silver hair knotted into a stern bun. She wore her spectacles at the very edge of her nose and stood straight with an imposing air. Her eyes seemed watchful and analytical, and Tracy felt them travel up and down her body as she approached with a forced smile.

"Hello," said Tracy. "I'd like a room, please."

"Of course," the woman replied, her voice as saccharine as her gaze was penetrating. She handed Tracy a form. "Just fill this in for me. And I'll need to see some ID, of course."

Tracy scribbled her details on the paper and handed it back along with her driver's license. The woman looked the license over with a furrowed brow.

"You're a long way from home, aren't you?"

"I'm just traveling," Tracy said. She hesitated for a moment before finally asking, "Can you tell me how to get to Madelyn Duncan's place?"

The woman looked up, and her pleasant demeanor dropped away.

"Why on Earth would you want to go out there?"

Tracy shrugged.

"We have some business matters to discuss."

The old woman looked at her and furrowed her brow.

"That right?"

Tracy nodded, her face straining to hold a look of polite innocence.

"She don't live in town," said the woman. "She lives off the beaten path, out in the deep low country. Likes to keep to herself."

"Well, she's expecting me," Tracy lied.

The woman scrutinized Tracy a little longer. Then, she sighed and scribbled some directions. Tracy smiled as she collected the strip of paper.

"Thank you."

The woman raised her eyebrows.

"Take care," she said. "She's a difficult woman even on her best day. And she recently lost her daughter, I'm sad to say."

Tracy nodded.

"Sure. I understand."

The woman watched as Tracy took her room key and made her way up to the second level. Finally free of that piercing gaze, Tracy sighed and walked down a slender hallway until she found the room number. When she opened the door, a musty smell stung her nose, and she sighed again as she tossed her bag on a small bed.

She looked around and put her hands on her hips while contemplating how many nights she'd have to spend in the tiny space. Then, she walked over to the window and pulled away the curtain.

Outside, the dying sun cast a dark hue over the town, the locals moving toward their cars as the businesses closed for the day.

Down below, amid the descending veil of dusk, she saw that the hotel proprietor had fled her desk and was now standing along the edge of the street, where she spoke to a man wearing a cowboy hat and a sheriff's badge. Tracy watched as they engaged in an animated conversation, their expressions obscured by the dimming twilight.

And then, the woman raised her hand and pointed up to Tracy's room.

Tracy almost flinched as the sheriff's gaze followed the woman's outstretched finger toward her window. But just before they locked eyes, she let the curtain fall and retreated back into the little claustrophobic space, where she spent the night tossing and turning amid the scent of old mothballs and the low hum of the ice machine in the hall.

Chapter 3

Tracy woke early the next day and got to work. As the sun pinked the pavement, she was already out and about, moving in and out of local businesses, confronting locals with direct questions that brought stuttering, hesitant responses.

At a little diner, she asked a waitress about Caroline's friends and acquaintances. The young woman responded by wrinkling her forehead and shrugging, her face looking tense as she refilled Tracy's coffee cup and walked back into the kitchen.

Elsewhere, it was more of the same. The cashier at the hardware store said he'd seen Caroline around but hadn't much reason to talk to her. The local barber said he'd known the girl's mother back in high school but hadn't seen much of her in recent years.

As the day progressed, Tracy found herself at a little bait shop. There, one of the employees said the girl's father had died years ago in an accident up at the quarry.

"And when was this?" asked Tracy as she pulled out a little notebook.

The young man opened his mouth and then paused as his boss approached. This was an old, gruff man in soiled overalls. He held a toothpick in one side of his mouth, and he tongued it over to the other side as he looked Tracy up and down.

"Johnny," he said. "Go on back and check the live wells."

The young man nodded and walked away. The bait shop owner watched him walk off and then turned his bulbous eyes on Tracy.

"Who are you, now?" he asked, his sunburned brow wrinkling up as he dumped a bucket of small minnows into what looked like a long metal trough.

"My name is Tracy."

"And what's all these questions for?" he asked, as the toothpick bobbed with each word.

Tracy looked behind her, where a pair of unwashed men appeared to be watching her from the back. She stared at them, and they turned toward a shelf of fishing tackle.

She took a breath, and the smell of dead fish wormed up into her nostrils.

"I'm sure you're aware that Caroline was killed last week," she told the bait shop owner.

The old man set his empty bucket down.

"I heard somethin about it. But it ain't really none of my business."

Tracy furrowed her brows.

"A murder in your town isn't cause for concern?"

He pushed his bottom lip out and shrugged.

"You wanna buy some bait?"

She left the little shop and stepped out into the fresh air. She watched the people as they moved about, their heads pointed down while they passed one another in silence. She assessed them thoughtfully, her brow bunched up as she frowned.

This was nothing like the quaint small towns from the movies, where politeness and charm were woven into the fabric of everyday life. There were no warm smiles nor heartfelt hellos. People moved about like jaded urban dwellers with hard hearts and deeply private thoughts.

By early afternoon, she was driving away and happy for it. On the outskirts of Reedsville in the dense low country, Caroline's mother had a small home amid the thicket and solitude. The proprietor of the Blue Bonnet had drawn a little map, and Tracy held it up as she drove, her eyes flicking from the paper to the pockmarked road, which hadn't been serviced in years.

After about twenty minutes, she pulled off the main road and onto a ragged path. The tires crunched on the gravelly ground as it wound its way into the thick embrace of the endless, tangled woods.

She looked around as the tires bounced against the uneven path. Sparse, dilapidated fences ran along the edges, their weather-beaten pickets barely standing against the heavy weight of vines and knotted creepers. Beyond them, intermittent fields lay fallow, the soil scarred with the remnants of old crops now replaced by wild grasses, golden and swaying in the late afternoon sunlight.

Tracy eyed them with a frown and then returned her gaze to the road. Up ahead, the path bent into a rounded hook, where an ancient oak tree, knotted and gnarled, stood crooked at the curve, its few remaining leaves fluttering in the humid southern breeze.

She slowed and eased her car into the turn, the carriage jostling as the tires bit into the weather-beaten road. She drove on, her vehicle dipping in and out of great pooling shadows, where the tall, smothering trees blotted out the high-away sun.

After a few minutes, the house finally came into view, hints of white showing intermittently through the thick vegetative overgrowth. As Tracy drove closer, the structure revealed itself in all its melancholy glory. Not quite ramshackled, it was decades past its prime. Shingles peeled away from the roof like scales from some enormous dying beast. Windows, dusty and water-stained, gazed out onto the wilderness like hollow, empty eyes, while the paint, once vibrant white, now flaked away from the old wood siding, which was warped and grayed by all the long years.

As she rolled closer, Tracy saw an old birdbath standing lopsided in the overgrown yard, its cement bowl empty and stained by calcified bird droppings. Around the house, weeds burst forth from cracks in the driveway, which held an old rusted car with one flat tire.

Tracy parked and stepped outside amid the chittering of cicadas. She looked up at the porch, where an old rocking chair creaked in the breeze. She glanced at a window, and someone pulled back, a bright red curtain falling as they retreated into the house.

Tracy took a deep breath and stepped up onto the wood porch, which groaned and whined with every step. Next to the rocking chair sat an old two-liter bottle of diet soda, its insides packed full of old wet cigarette butts. Tracy's lip curled as she rapped her knuckle against the door.

She waited and listened to the sound of shuffling feet on the other side. Then, she forced a polite smile as the door opened to reveal a middle-aged woman in a soiled bathrobe.

The woman coughed as she looked at Tracy, and something vile broke loose from the back of her throat. Tracy subdued a cringe as the woman swallowed the ball of mucus.

"Hello," she said as the woman cleared her throat. "Are you Ms. Duncan?"

The woman looked Tracy up and down, her wrinkled face twisted into a scowl.

"Who wants to know?"

The words spilled from her mouth slowly, each one bent by a thick Southern accent. Tracy molded her expression into one of innocent politeness. Or, at least, she hoped."

"My name is Tracy Sterling."

The woman looked her over again and put a hand on her wide hips.

"What's your business out here?"

"Well," said Tracy. "I'm an investigator, and I was hoping I could ask you a few quest—"

The woman's face turned even more sour.

"I already said all I got to say when the sheriff come out. There ain't nothin more to talk about. What's done is done."

Tracy started to speak but paused at the sight of a young man of about 17 or maybe 19 lingering in the space behind the woman. Ms. Duncan followed Tracy's eyes and turned.

"Get on out of here," she told the young man. "This don't concern you."

Tracy watched as the young man retreated into the other room.

"Ma'am," she started, but the woman raised a hand.

"You need to get in your car and get off my land," she said. "I don't have nothin to tell you. You're wasting both our time."

Tracy opened her mouth to say more, but the door had already slammed shut in her face. She stepped back and gave the house one last look. Then, she turned and walked off the porch.

About an hour later, she drove down another bad road, this one cutting into the woods on the other side of the small town. Howard had given her a map with the location of Caroline's murder, and she hoped to get a look at the place before dark.

Ahead, the barren road pushed into a wild expanse of marshland, the undulating terrain painted in varying shades of mossy green that was speckled here and there with sporadic blooms of red and orange wildflowers. On one side of the road, a shallow creek meandered lazily, its murky water winking in the dying light. Deeper still, beyond the marshes and through a veil of Spanish moss, a thick mass of cypress trees towered, their tops disappearing into the twilight.

Tracy pulled before them and parked at the side of the road. There was a little dirt trail running alongside the muddy creek, and it cut into the woods, disappearing beneath the dark canopy. She looked at it for several minutes before finally killing the engine and stepping out of the car.

Fireflies began their evening dance, their tiny lights flickering like stars in the approaching night. She looked around, but there was no one to see.

She shut the car door and started up the trail. Croaking frogs leaped into the boggy creek waters at the sound of her crunching shoes, while the sun hung low in the sky, casting long, tremulous shadows that danced through the skeletal reeds lining the path.

As Tracy moved, the reeds whispered in the breeze, their brittle heads rustling in a somber serenade as twilight descended upon the swamp. A soup of humidity hung heavy in the air, and her shirt clung against her sweaty skin. A pervasive, sour scent wormed its way up her nostrils, the smell of decay lying beneath the lush veneer of the marshland, clawing at her senses with every inhalation.

Up the trail she went, the deafening quiet screaming in her ears, as her hand involuntarily traced her holstered gun. She bent under a low-hanging branch and emerged from the trail into a small clearing. Before her, the murky waters of a large pond stretched blackly, its still waters reflecting the changing colors in a false inverted sky.

Tracy approached the pond and looked around. Green, pockmarked lily pads floated lazily on the surface, while gnarled roots clawed at the banks. It was quiet except for the sound of cicadas and a mournful bird, its cries echoing across the water. An unseen twin returned its call. Tracy turned toward the sound and saw the dock. She looked at it. Assessed its rickety wood posts. She smelled the stifling air.

A big bullfrog croaked as she made her way to the structure, which made a wobbly pier out over the water. She stepped onto it, and the old gray wood groaned and creaked. Still, she walked, half expecting her foot to punch through one of the rotten planks, until at last she reached the end.

She knelt there, the moss-dampened planks pressing into her knees. She extended a hand to the water. Her fingers hovered above the mirror-like surface, her reflection staring back at her in an echo of shared despair. She could almost sense the cold terror that had once gripped the victim, the chilling dread that leached away hope and life.

The murkiness of the water whispered the horrors of the young woman's final moments. The desperation of her struggle was all too easy to envision. The futile battle against the stagnant waters, her cries echoing unheard in the silence of the swamp.

As evening set in, the marsh came alive. Mosquitoes ate her. Bullfrogs croaked along the banks. There was a big rustle in the reeds as a water rat scurried into the shallows.

The dock groaned as someone approached from behind.

Tracy withdrew her weapon and spun around. A young man stood before her, the same one who had been eavesdropping behind Ms. Duncan an hour before. He stopped and held up his hands.

"I'm sorry," he said. "I didn't mean to startle you."

Tracy lowered her weapon.

"That's a good way to get shot."

"I'm sorry," he said.

Tracy put the gun away and looked him over. He was thin and about average height. He wore a tight black t-shirt with the logo of some heavy metal band Tracy didn't recognize. And he watched her with dark brown eyes that peered out from below his long, disheveled black bangs. He looked like someone who didn't belong in this part of the world. Or like someone trying hard to hide the fact that they did.

"Are you Caroline's brother?"

He nodded.

"My name's Carter."

Tracy nodded.

"And what are you doing here, Carter?"

He took a step toward her.

"I thought I might find you here."

His voice was steady, almost monotone, devoid of emotion. Not happy, angry or sad.

"Why?" she asked.

He shrugged.

"Just a hunch."

She nodded.

"Maybe you should be an investigator," she said.

He tilted his head at her.

"Why are you really out here?" he asked.

"I'm investigating your sister's murder."

"But you're not a cop," he said matter of factly.

Tracy furrowed her brow.

"What makes you say that?"

"I searched your name on the internet," he said. "After you finished talking to my mom."

"And what did you read?"

He shrugged.

"That you used to be a cop. But then you quit and became a private investigator."

Tracy nodded.

"All true."

The young man looked at her with no expression, and Tracy began to wonder if he might be high.

"So, who hired you?" he asked. "I mean, you're obviously not investigating Caroline's murder for the police. So, who are you working for?"

Tracy thought for a moment and then answered.

"I was hired by Peter Teller's lawyer."

The young man furrowed his brows a little.

"You don't think he killed my sister?"

"I don't know," said Tracy. "I'm trying to find out."

Carter shook his head.

"You're off to a bad start. My mom won't help you. Even if you did work for the cops. She won't talk to you."

"Why not?" asked Tracy.

He looked at her as if she were a young child asking why water is wet.

"Because she's afraid. Everyone around here is."

Tracy took a step toward him, and the dock groaned its complaints.

"Afraid of what?"

"It's not what," said Carter. "It's who."

"Afraid of whom then?"

The young man furrowed his brow.

"The Parker family."

"And who's that?" asked Tracy.

Carter seemed to restrain a chuckle.

"You really did just get into town. The Parker family runs everything around here. They own the quarry. They provide all the jobs. Everything runs through them. And they run everything."

Tracy frowned at him.

"And your mom is afraid of them, why? Have they threatened your family?"

He shook his head slowly, his dark eyes never leaving hers.

"They don't threaten. Not with words, at least. But everyone around here knows the deal. You don't talk to outsiders. You don't disrupt the way things are. You don't mess with the status quo."

"But you're talking to me," said Tracy. "You're not scared?"

He broke eye contact for the first time and looked up at the sky, where the clouds burned orange amid the fire of the setting sun. The wind kicked up, and a few birds fled the swaying trees.

"Maybe," he said. "But I won't be here much longer."

"Why not?" asked Tracy.

He looked at her.

"I'm leaving for college."

"That's good," said Tracy.

He nodded.

"You have no idea. I hate this place. I hate everything about it. I can't wait to leave."

She nodded.

"I can imagine."

He firmed his mouth and approached until they were face to face. Tracy turned slightly and allowed him to pass. He proceeded to the end of the dock and paused. Tracy watched as he stared down into the water, his eyes flaring slightly as his rippling reflection stared back.

"Were you and your sister close?" she asked as she eyed him from behind.

"Not really," he said. "This is where they found her?"

"Yes."

"Did she suffer?"

"I don't know," said Tracy. "I think maybe yes."

They stood in silence while bullfrogs croaked at the edges of the pond. Insects joined the chorus as the sun continued to fail, and Tracy was struck by how quickly things turned dark amid the swallowing tangles of the swampland forest.

The young man stared at the water as if lost in a trance.

29

"Carter," Tracy said softly. "Is there anything you can tell me? Did your sister have enemies? Is there anyone else who might have wanted to hurt her?"

The young man shook his head without turning around.

"I don't know," he said. "But there is someone who might know."

"Who?"

"A girl named Maddie Taylor. She and Caroline hung out a lot. They were close."

"I'll talk to her."

Carter turned around, his dark eyes the same as before. Dry.

"She may not want to talk to you," he said. "She won't want to get on the wrong side of the Parker family. She knows the deal like everyone else."

Tracy nodded.

"I'll try anyway."

He nodded and walked back up the dock, his hands in his jeans pockets as his feet made the old wood whine.

"Carter," said Tracy.

He stopped and turned.

"How can I get in touch with you?"

He shrugged.

"I'll find you."

She nodded, and they looked at each other a while longer, the sun now just a boiling red fingernail as it sank beneath the top of the stifling forest.

"You're not going to like it here," he said.

And with that, he turned and walked up the trail.

Chapter 4

Tracy found Maddie Taylor later in the night at the local bar. A sprawling billiard and dance hall, the place was nearly the size of a small warehouse. It also seemed like the only real entertainment in town—and not just in recent years. To Tracy's eyes, the old wooden building looked like it had survived a hundred summers and just as many storms. And she eyed the foundations doubtfully as she approached the aging structure.

Music met her ears long before she reached the doors to the establishment, its neon sign buzzing and flickering amid the hot and humid southern summer night. As she approached the entrance, a pair of giggling young girls stepped outside, their skin soft and fair, eyes large and blue. Tracy gave them a nod that was not reciprocated. Then, she pushed the door open and stepped inside.

She paused in the entryway and looked around. The twang of country music melded with the clink of glasses and deep, throaty laughter that permeated the smoky air. Instantly, she felt the collective gaze of the room focus on her like a spotlight. The barroom chatter faltered momentarily, curious and suspicious eyes scanning her unfamiliar face before returning to their drinks and conversations, leaving only the faintest undercurrent of unease.

Across the room, bathed in the amber glow of dimmed lights, patrons leaned against the worn-out bar. Tracy maneuvered through the small crowd, as the scent of stale beer, fried food and cheap perfume wafted through the air. She slipped onto a stool at the end of the bar, gestured for the barman and ordered a beer. The grizzled man had a prominent paunch and thinning hair, and his mustache twitched as he drew a cold beer from the tap.

He slid the frosted glass toward her, and she paid him in cash. He collected the money and turned away, while Tracy sipped the beer and looked around the bar.

In one far corner, a young man in a cowboy hat clung to a frenzied mechanical bull, his body convulsing in a desperate dance with gravity as onlookers cheered and jeered in equal measure. At the other end of the place, couples moved rhythmically to the slow drawl of country music, their boots stirring up ghosts of sawdust from atop a wooden floor worn smooth by traffic and time.

Not far away, a group of young men played billiards with a pair of perky-looking girls who blinked at them with big bashful eyes. Even amid all the clatter and noise, these men stood out, their voices booming with arrogance and expletives, the sharp crack of the billiard balls punctuating their brash laughter.

Tracy turned her head and watched them. The three men were decorated with tattoos, absurd in design and vibrant in color. With each movement, their muscular bodies twitched beneath their t-shirts, which seemed at least a size too small. By accident or intent, who could say?

And then, she noticed Maddie Taylor. A figure distinct in the crowd, the girl sat at a table nestled in the back, sipping a drink with a friend. Tracy immediately recognized her from her social media photos, a godsend for any PI who needed to match a name to a face. She casually picked up her own drink, slid off the bar stool, and made her way across the floor.

"Hello," she said as she approached the table. "You're Maddie Taylor, aren't you?"

The young woman looked up.

"Huh?"

Tracy smiled.

"My name is Tracy. Do you mind if we talk?"

The two friends exchanged looks.

"Do I know you?" asked Maddie as she looked up at Tracy.

She was pretty in a plain sort of way. Or she would have been if she hadn't been wearing so much makeup. Her oily hair could use a good wash, too, Tracy thought.

"No," said Tracy with a bright smile. "But I was hoping you could help me with something."

The girl wrinkled up her forehead.

"Help you with what?"

She said help like "hep" and you like "ya," and Tracy was reasonably sure she would say can't like "cain't" when she eventually told her she couldn't talk about Caroline's murder.

Tracy frowned over at the friend, a red-haired girl with a pair of thick thighs.

"It's kind of a private matter."

The friend gave her a long look and then stood up.

"I'll be at the bar," she said to Maddie as she walked away.

The girl watched her friend walk away and then watched as Tracy sat down at the table.

"Wow, this place is great," said Tracy as she looked around.

On the other side of the great room, a new victim held tight to the twisting mechanical bull, while the men over at the billiards table barked laughter.

"Yeah, I guess," said Maddie. "Who are you again?"

"My name is Tracy, and I'm trying to gather some facts on Caroline Duncan."

The girl's face turned somber.

"Oh," she said as she looked around.

Tracy gave her a consoling frown.

"I'm very sorry for your loss," she said. "I heard you two were good friends."

Maddie frowned as she looked around.

"Yeah."

Tracy followed her eyes to the men at the billiards table, who now seemed to be harassing a buxom waitress.

"Is everything ok?" asked Tracy.

The girl's eyes flicked to Tracy's."

"Sure," she said. "It's just. I don't really wanna talk about Caroline. It hurts too much, you know?"

Tracy narrowed her eyes a little and then brightened her face into a sympathetic smile.

"I do understand," she said. "However, I'm trying to make sure the perpetrator faces justice."

The girl's face turned inquisitive.

"Are you a cop or something?"

"No," said Tracy. "I'm a professional investigator who's been hired to look into the matter. I'm sad to say that the police aren't always as thorough as they should be. And I'm just making sure we don't overlook any important details."

The girl swallowed hard, and her eyes glanced back toward the billiards room.

"I can't talk to you. I want to, but I can't. Not here, at least."

Tracy sat back in her chair and raised her eyebrows.

"Why not?"

Her eyes flicked over to the men at the billiards tables.

"You see them boys over there playin pool? The ones makin all that noise? The big one's Beaux Parker. His daddy has a lot of pull in this town. If he sees me talking to you, he may tell his daddy. It could make trouble for me and my family."

Tracy kept her eyes on the girl.

"Why would they care if you talk to me? Do you think they had something to do with Caroline's murder?"

Maddie's eyes flicked over to Tracy's

"What? No. I mean, I don't think—"

"Well, what do we have here?" said a booming voice from behind.

Tracy felt it before she heard it – the oscillating shift of energy as the men from the billiards table approached from behind. Even still, she kept her eyes on the girl, whose throat buckled noticeably as she swallowed hard.

"Hey, Maddie. Who's your friend?"

The smell of cheap cologne wafted over and stung Tracy's nose. She looked up to her left, where Beaux Parker stood with his friends. They were all big young men, but he was the biggest by far. He wore a tight black t-shirt that did little to conceal his muscled frame. His face was handsome. And the sneer on his lips said he knew it. And his deep brown eyes devoured Tracy and the world as if they were all a part of his domain.

"She's a pretty one," he said as he leered down at Tracy.

Maddie shrugged.

"She ain't no friend of mine," said the girl in her twangy southern accent. "I just now met her tonight."

"That right?" said Beaux. "Well, now, I wouldn't mind gettin acquainted with her myself."

His voice deepened as he said the words, and he assessed Tracy's body with a lewd gaze.

Tracy stared up at him with a hard glare.

"I don't know, Beaux," said one of his friends. "She looks liable to bite."

Beaux shook his head as a big oily grin consumed the whole of his face.

"Oh, don't you worry now. I know how to tame wild phillies like this one. You just gotta dig your spurs in real deep."

He glanced back at his friends, who all traded smiles.

Tracy pushed her lip out and looked directly at the young man's crotch, which was eye level, about a foot from her face.

"I don't know," she said. "Your spur looks a little modest from where I'm sitting."

Beaux's face changed color as his friends stifled laughter.

"Ha ha," he said with a sarcastic tone. "You're pretty funny. You're also clearly not from these parts."

Tracy looked up into his eyes and shook her head.

"Nope."

The young man frowned.

"Whereabouts are you from?"

Tracy shrugged without breaking eye contact, her face an unyielding mask of indifference.

"Someplace else."

Beaux smiled at her, or sneered. Whatever it was, the gesture showed his teeth.

"You're a little smart ass. Aren't you? Maybe I oughta drag you outside and show you some manners."

The young man's friends laughed. Maddie swallowed hard as she looked back and forth between Tracy and Beaux.

"Leave her alone, Beaux. She ain't from here. She don't know how things are."

"Shut up," he said, his eyes never breaking from Tracy's. "She don't know yet. But she's fixin to find out."

All eyes fell on Tracy, who raised her eyebrows and looked down at the floor. She took a deep breath and slowly got to her feet. Then, with a sudden movement, she took hold of Beaux's muscled shoulders and drove her knee into his testicles.

As if they shared a common weakness, the young man's friends all grimaced and flinched backward. A little yelp slipped from Beaux's mouth, and the bar fell silent as he collapsed down onto one knee.

Without pausing, Tracy pushed her way past the other two men and made her way toward the exit. The other patrons watched in stunned silence as she crossed the room and exited the building.

She let the doors fall shut behind her and paused to take a breath. Outside, it was mostly dark, except for a few sparse lampposts that splashed puddles of weak light up and down the street.

She stepped amid the humid air and crossed into the road just as the doors opened violently behind her.

"Hey!" said a harsh male voice.

She turned and stood amid the middle of the barren street, while the three men tumbled out of the bar. They approached and swelled before her, their forms dark silhouettes against the dimly lit street. Beaux limped slightly as he centered himself between his friends.

"You're fucking dead," he spat.

Tracy squared herself before them, her eyes darting from one to another. Her fingers flexed at her sides, adrenaline coursing through her veins as she prepared for a long-shot fight she should have seen coming a mile away.

As her eyes darted over the men, their predatory grins grew wide, eyes glistening with malevolent glee in the faint light. As she took a step back, they spread before her, the tension hanging thick, a tinderbox waiting for a spark.

"You have no clue who you fucked with tonight," said Beaux.

Molding his face into a gargolyian grin, the young man stepped toward her and pulled up his shirt, revealing a set of chiseled abdominal muscles and a pistol wedged in the waistband of his jeans.

Without hesitating, Tracy reached forward and plucked the weapon free. In one fluid motion, she brought the but of the gun down hard on Beaux's forehead and watched as he staggered backward like a man struggling for balance atop the deck of a shifting boat.

The other men watched with mute astonishment as Beaux collapsed backward onto the pavement. They looked at their fallen friend for a moment as he clutched his face. Then, their eyes flicked up to Tracy, who looked the pistol over and then tossed it a few feet away.

"Holy shit," said one of the men.

Beaux shook the cobwebs from his head and slowly climbed to his feet. He staggered about for a few seconds on wobbly legs, a big red welt growing on his head by the second. He looked at her, his eyes unfocused and blinking as his woozy mind came back online. Then, his face flared red, and his eyes sharpened as he stared at Tracy with white-hot rage.

"You're fucking dead," he hissed as he took a step forward.

As if they'd practiced the maneuver a hundred times before, the other men spread out and surrounded Tracy, their thick muscled chests expanding with every hateful breath as they clenched their fists at their sides.

While they spread before her, Tracy felt the sickening sensation of being cornered, and her fingers began to move toward her pistol as their bodies formed a human barricade.

"That's enough, Beaux," came a gruff voice from the shadows.

They all turned as the sheriff appeared from the darkness.

The young man flashed his teeth and continued staring at Tracy, his eyes aflame with hate as they bored into hers.

"She came at me first, Sheriff."

Tracy shook her head slowly without taking her eyes from his.

"Horse shit," she said.

The sheriff stepped closer.

"Enough," he said with a voice that echoed off the buildings. "You boys get on out of here. I'll take care of this."

Tracy continued staring at Beaux, who had begun to retreat a few steps.

"I'll be seeing you again real soon," he said, his eyes flaring as he spoke.

"That's enough now, Beaux," said the sheriff. "Don't make me go and call your daddy."

Tracy watched as the three young men turned and walked away. When they were gone, she turned to the sheriff and looked him over. He appeared to be in his mid-fifties, but his physique indicated a youth of physical labor or athletics. He had a strong jaw and pale blue eyes, and he wore a cowboy hat that he pulled off better than anyone Tracy had ever seen.

"Now, miss," he said. "I'm gonna have to ask you to come with me."

"Why?" asked Tracy. "Am I under arrest?"

The sheriff frowned.

"Come on, now," he said. "There ain't no reason for all that. I just want to talk to you a little bit."

He turned and held a hand toward his police cruiser parked several spaces down the road. It was a sleek Dodge Charger that looked almost like a spacecraft amid the rest of the town. Tracy shook her head and made her way to the vehicle.

About fifteen minutes later, she sat across from the sheriff while he looked her over from the other side of his desk. His office was modest and relatively neat. All around, the walls were decorated with pictures of him shaking hands with the important people of the town or holding huge fish with those same people as they all grinned back at the camera.

"Now," he said as he leaned back in his squeaking chair, "I don't know how things is done up north. But normally, in this state, it's customary for private investigators to notify local law enforcement when they're in town investigatin a case."

Tracy raised her eyebrows.

"I've only been here a day."

The sheriff raised his eyebrows.

"And what a day it's been. In just 24 hours, you managed to cause a whole bevy of trouble. That's sayin somethin."

Tracy shook her head.

"I didn't cause anything. I was having a polite conversation, and those men began harassing me. It was completely unprovoked."

"Mm hm," said the sheriff. "And who exactly were you conversatin with?"

"That's my business," said Tracy.

The sheriff frowned.

"Is it now?"

Tracy gave an exasperated sigh.

"I'll tell you what, Sheriff. I'll answer your questions if you answer mine."

He almost chuckled.

"Is that right?" he said. "Alright. You go ahead and ask your little questions. We'll see if I feel like answering."

"Why did you arrest Peter Teller for the murder of Caroline Duncan?"

"Cause he's guilty as hell," said the sheriff. "That's why."

Tracy turned one of her palms upward.

"How do you know? What evidence do you have?"

The sheriff gave her a hard look.

"Listen, here, young miss. I don't need to tell you nothin. But just for the sake of it, I'll go ahead and let you know that we had two witnesses that saw him leave the Blue Bonnet during the window of the murder. And the proprietor of the hotel said she'd heard the two of them fightin up a storm just about every night they been there. That enough for you?"

She shook her head.

"Not in the least."

He firmed his mouth.

"Well, there's more. But I ain't fixin to tip the DA's hand."

"Can I talk to these witnesses?" asked Tracy.

'No, you may not. At least not with my help."

She shrugged.

"Well, then. I guess we're done here."

He leaned forward.

"Not quite." He lowered his eyebrows and sucked his teeth. "You need to listen to me. Not just cause I want you to. But for your own sake. This place you're in right now. It ain't no New York City. People here keep to themselves. They like the peace and quiet. They don't like outsiders stirrin up trouble. They don't respond to that sort of thing kindly."

Tracy gave him a bored look.

"I'm not here to cause trouble. I'm just here to gather facts."

The sheriff shook his head.

"It don't make no difference. The longer you're here, the more trouble there will be. It's just the way it is.

She returned his gaze as she leaned forward a little.

"And who'll be causing this trouble?" she asked. "The Parker family?"

He narrowed his eyes, and his face seemed to darken.

"Listen to me," he said. "Your boy, this Peter fellow, he's guilty. You can bet on it. There ain't no need for you to be pokin around here. Now, tonight you run up into some real trouble, even if you don't know it. And you were damn lucky I come up on you when I did. I might not be there next time."

Tracy stood.

"I'll take my chances. Thanks for the help, though."

She turned and walked toward the door.

"Ms. Sterling," he said as she reached for the door.

39

Tracy paused and turned.

"You best remember what I said. I read up on you online. I know you're well-accomplished for your age. And you may be somethin special where you're from. But here, in this place, things are different. And if you ain't careful, you gonna find that out the hard way."

Tracy looked at him and shook her head.

"Things are the same everywhere. Just greedy people trying to hide their lies."

With that, she walked out the door and back out into the night, where the street lay black and barren in the hot and sticky summer night.

Chapter 5

Tracy awoke to knocking. She sat up and blinked as the world crystallized. She shook the sleep from her head and looked at her pistol on the nightstand next to her bed.

More knocking, this time harder.

"Just a minute," she said as she threw the covers away.

She got to her feet and put on a robe. Then, she collected her gun and moved to the door, which rattled in its frame as a big fist thundered against it on the other side.

"Who is it?" she said.

It was quiet for a moment, and then a deep voice spoke.

"We're here on behalf of Bill Parker," it said. "Can we talk?"

Almost instinctively, she took a step back. Then, she shook the sleep from her head and set her gun on the dresser.

"Give me a minute."

She dressed quickly and straightened her hair in front of the mirror. Then, she opened the door a crack and looked out into the hall. There, stood a pair of burly men with forearms like small trees. They wore jeans and flannel shirts with the sleeves rolled up halfway. Their bearded faces regarded her with mute indifference as they looked at her through the crack.

"You that PI?" one asked.

She narrowed her eyes.

"Yeah."

The big man nodded.

"Our boss wants a word with you."

She opened the door.

"When?"

They both looked at her like she was dense.

"Right now."

She frowned at this.

"Where?"

"Up at the quarry," the same man said. "He don't leave that place ever."

She sighed.

"Alright."

They stepped back as if to give her room.

"We'll drive you up there."

Tracy almost laughed.

"That's ok," she said. "I'll follow you in my car."

The man scratched his big, square jaw while his mute partner looked on.

"Suit yourself."

Soon after, she found herself following the men's large SUV through the early morning town. The streets were already busy with foot traffic. And both vehicles slowed at intersections to wait for people to cross. Then, they headed toward the thick forest outskirts, where civilization gave way to the tangles of nature.

As she drove, Tracy observed the slow transition from sleepy town to dense forest. After another 20 minutes, her jaw dropped as the seemingly impenetrable thicket turned into a barren landscape that looked to have been wiped by a great furnace or perhaps a nuclear bomb.

Verdant greens gave way to harsh browns and a desolate stretch of dirt that bore the scars of incessant excavation. On the horizon, the unending chasm of the Parker family's quarry appeared, a gaping maw in the once beautiful landscape.

Driving towards the quarry, the scene gradually changed from a dull, empty panorama to a hive of activity. Machines roared in the distance, as men moved about like bees around a disrupted hive, each one scurrying under the weight of his respective task.

And amid the vibration of activity stood a balding figure perched high up on a hill overlooking the quarry, like some king of nothing surveying his scarred and smoking domain.

Bill Parker was unmistakable. Dressed in jeans, he wore a gold belt buckle that gleamed ostentatiously against the morning light. His crisp dress shirt pressed tight against his protruding stomach, and his sleeves were rolled up to reveal meaty forearms that hinted at a formidable youth. His bald head caught the glint of the rising sun as he stared over the vast cavity his empire had gouged from the earth.

Beneath him, the quarry stretched out like a vision of purgatory, a stark scar against the natural splendor of the land. Below, great machines relentlessly gnawed at the earth, their metallic jaws opening and closing as they stripped away its skin and probed deep with its guts.

Within the billowing dust, workers moved like ghostly apparitions, their figures barely distinguishable in the early morning light. And all the while, their lord watched with a judging gaze, which didn't veer even as Tracy approached.

As she settled a few feet away from him, the two big men fell back a few feet, their hands crossed over their waists as if they meant to shield their genitals from a possible assault.

Tracy looked back at them and then let her eyes settle on Bill Parker, who flexed his jaw as he spat onto the parched dirt.

"So, you're the private eye that's been pokin her nose everwhere."

Tracy nodded.

"I guess so." She raised her eyebrows at him. "And you're the famous Bill Parker I've heard so much about?"

He leaned over and spat again.

"Yes, ma'am."

He jerked his chin at the two big men, and they walked away. Tracy looked out over the quarry.

"And this is all yours," she said.

He followed her eyes to the great cleave in the earth.

"Yes, it is."

She shook her head.

"It looks like hell."

He almost laughed.

"It's money is what it is."

She looked around.

"It just looks like dirt and rocks to me."

He shook his head as his lip curled into a condescending sneer.

43

"Dirt and rocks," he repeated as he shook his head. "Well, I guess that's what someone like you would see, bein where you're from."

He looked at her, an amused smirk on his old, weathered face.

"This here ain't no simple rock quarry despite what you see. You'd do better to think of it as a gold mine."

The man's eyes sparkled with a shrewd intensity, his Southern drawl liquid as it laced every word in a subtle twang. He kicked at a rock with the toe of his boot, sending it skittering down into the quarry floor.

"Ya see, this ain't just any ol' quarry. It's a granite quarry. The king of stones, the real money-maker. You see them sparkly bits in there?" He pointed the toe of his boot at a chunk of rock on the ground. "That's quartz and feldspar mixed in with a touch of mica. Gives it this strong and gorgeous look, real high-end stuff. That's why city folks like you love it for all your countertops and fancy floorings."

He gestured toward a few massive slabs of stone waiting to be hauled away.

"But it ain't just about looking pretty. No, ma'am. This shit is tougher than nails. It's resistant to heat, scratches, you name it. Makes it perfect for kitchens, bathrooms, even fireplaces. People pay a pretty penny for that kind of durability."

He leaned in closer, his breath smelling of coffee and cigarettes as his voice dropped to a conspiratorial whisper.

"But here's the real kicker. Granite's got status. Owning a granite countertop or a granite bathroom is a statement. Tells the world you've got the cash to spend on the good stuff. And in this world, image is everything. People will pay through the nose just to show off."

Straightening up, he spread his arms wide, encompassing the expanse of the quarry.

"Every chunk of granite we pull outta this earth is potential money in the bank. It's a commodity, like oil or gold. And the best part? As long as there are folks with money to burn, there's gonna be a demand for the stuff."

His grin was sharp as a razor as he clapped his hands together, dust flying from the impact.

"So you see, Ms. Sterling, this here quarry ain't just a hole in the ground. It's a constant flow of cold, hard cash. And I intend to squeeze every last penny out of it."

She sucked in a breath.

"Good for you. Is that why I'm here? To talk about rocks?"

He glowered at her, and she thought she saw a hint of malice in his bulbous eyes.

"I'm not finished," he said. "There's something else out here besides just granite."

He looked around and sniffed the air, like an animal taking in the scent of a female in heat. She lowered her eyebrows as his eyes darted about in a mock search.

"What?" she asked.

His eyes finally landed on her, and he showed his teeth a little.

"Something better. Better than granite. Better than gold even."

She tried to look bored.

"Why don't you enlighten me?"

He kicked at a clod of dirt.

"Well, you cain't see it is the thing. Cause it's in there real deep." He brought his boot up and slammed it down on the chunk of earth. It broke into pieces, and he swiveled his foot back and forth as he crushed it into small fragments. He looked up at her. "But it's in there."

Tracy gave an impatient sigh.

"What are you talking about?"

He reached into his pocket and removed a handkerchief. She watched as he ran it across his sweating brow.

"I'm talking about rare earth minerals. That's what."

She shook her head.

"Is this a geology lesson? Because I never had much interest, to be honest."

He gave her an amused look that bordered on pity.

"You may not have much interest in geology, but it's the foundation of your very life. Yours and everybody else's."

He reached down with a grunt and picked up one of the small dirt clogs.

"You see, the rare earth minerals I'm talking about ain't like your typical dirt. And they ain't actually all that rare, despite the name. No, ma'am. They're just hard to dig outta the ground, is all. Sparsely scattered, if you will."

He looked at her as he fondled the dirt clog, his fingers moving against it in an almost sexual way, as if he held no dirt at all but a woman's soft and supple breast. He grinned.

"Now," he said, "you might be wonderin why they're important? Well, let's start with that there smartphone in your pocket. Bet you a cold beer it's got some of them rare earth elements in there. Makes all them gadgets and doohickeys work just right. Why, there's even one called europium, gives your screen them bright red colors."

He raised his eyebrows.

"And you know all them big windmills you city folk love? The ones that generate all that clean electricity? They got a load of this stuff called neodymium in them. Makes mighty powerful magnets, helps them generate electricity out of thin air."

Looking thoughtful, he pushed his lower lip out.

"But it ain't all just phones and windmills. These here elements are important for the country's defense. Helps the military make everything from guided missiles to communication devices. Can't defend ourselves proper without them. Not no more, at least."

He paused and looked skyward, his eyes squinting up at the sun.

"Even beyond that, space, the final frontier as they call it, is gonna need these minerals. Every satellite up there, and anything else we want to put on Mars or the Moon, it's all gonna have to use these rare earth minerals."

He looked at her and frowned.

"Now, the trouble is, Ms. Sterling, most these minerals are over yonder in China. And that leaves us in a bit of a pickle, don't it? Means we gotta find them somewhere else."

He held his hands out toward the quarry as if to introduce it for the very first time.

"Out there is the answer. We started finding them about a year ago. All by accident. And you can imagine my reaction. Now, this place ain't just worth millions. It's worth billions."

He looked at her, and his eyes set in deep.

"Now, given all that, what do you think someone like me might do to protect a billion-dollar enterprise?"

She looked up at him and narrowed her eyes a little.

"Ah, now I see. This is all some kind of veiled threat."

He pushed out his lower lip.

"Call it what you like. I prefer to think of it as a courtesy. Or you can think of it as some helpful advice. If I were you, I'd wrap things up quick and go on home."

She shrugged.

"I have a job to do first. So, I'll probably be around a little longer than you like. Anyway, you've got me intrigued now with your little speech. Everyone seems so nervous about me asking questions. You included. Why is that?"

He scratched his jaw.

"I have big plans in the works. I've got a buyer who wants this quarry. It's the deal of a lifetime. And I don't need some big-city private investigator digging into my business or the business of my associates. Now, as I understand it, this girl that turned up dead, the sheriff's already made an arrest, and that book is closed. Ain't no need to keep picking at it. I'd prefer to see this matter over and done with."

Tracy gave a polite smile.

"Mr. Parker, I can appreciate your situation. And I'm really not very interested in your business or your dirty laundry or your shady connections or whatever it is you're concerned about. But I have been paid to do a job. And the book on that girl's murder is not closed. Not until I'm finished. When I am, I'll be out of your hair. But until then, I'm afraid you and your son and everyone else in this town are going to have to put up with me."

He looked at her and shook his head.

"First off," he said. "As far as my son goes, he's his own man. So, I can't take no responsibility for his actions. He's none too fond of you, from what I understand. My advice is to keep away from him. For your sake and for his. For everyone's."

She started to say something, but he spoke over her.

"Second, my advice stands. And you should take it. This ain't the city, Ms. Sterling. It's the country. The deep country. And it's a dangerous place, especially for someone like you. City people, they just ain't got the right kind of sense for a place like this. Why, they liable to be strollin through the woods and walk right into a gator's mouth. I've seen it happen. One second, they just lookin around at all the pretty trees and flowers. Then, next thing you know, somethin come right out the woods and take them down into the bog. No screamin or nothin. Just all quiet as they get sucked down into them black waters. Gone like that."

He crushed the dirt clog in his hand. He looked at her.

"Half the time, nothin's ever found. No body. No clothes. No nothin. They just vanish like God plucked them right up off the face of the Earth. But country folk. The ones that grew up around here. They know what happened. And them people, the ones that know, the ones that learned, they know to stay on the trail and keep out the woods. And that's how they stay safe."

He shook the dirt from his hand and let it fall to the ground.

"Now, in my mind, you've had fair warning, Ms. Sterling," he said. "So, you get on from here. Go on with your business. And think hard about what I said."

He turned his back to her just as the two men approached. Tracy looked at him for a moment longer, her sharp tongue nearly cutting her mouth as she held it behind the fence of her teeth. Then, without speaking, she turned and followed the men down the hill.

Chapter 6

When Tracy returned from the quarry, she found Howard sitting in the lobby of the hotel. Neatly dressed in a short-sleeve polo and a pair of black slacks, he sat on the room's one little sofa, his eyes pinched in concentration as he went through a stack of documents. Tracy paused in the entryway for a moment and glanced over to the front desk, where the proprietor was pretending not to study the lawyer as she wiped down the countertop for what had to be the hundredth time in the last 24 hours. Tracy shook her head and looked back at Howard, who seemed lost in a world of his own thoughts.

"Howard," she said.

He looked up and blinked at her.

"Hi there," he said.

Tracy approached.

"I wasn't expecting you."

He frowned at her.

"I wasn't expecting me either. Not until I got a call from the local sheriff."

She sighed and shook her head.

"Is that so?"

He nodded.

"What's going on?"

She looked back over her shoulder, and the proprietor dropped her head. She watched as the woman polished the crystal-clean counter with rough circular strokes.

"Not here," said Tracy. "Let's go upstairs."

He nodded and stood. He tucked his papers under his arm, and they made their way to Tracy's room. Once inside, he took a seat on a stiff little chair by the window and rubbed his tired eyes.

"How goes it on your end?" she asked.

"Well, he said. "I met with the DA. He's a prick, but aren't they all?" He looked up at her. "I'm more interested in what's going on down here. What was this about a bar fight?"

Tracy stifled a laugh.

"Is that what the sheriff said? That I got in a bar fight?"

Howard shrugged.

"More or less. He also said that you were harassing some of the locals. Making them feel uncomfortable."

Tracy shook her head.

"Is that so?"

Howard frowned.

"What's going on, Tracy?"

She sat on the edge of the bed.

"Well, your client wasn't kidding when he called the people here strange."

Howard furrowed his brow.

"How so?"

"They're all private, true enough. And suspicious of outsiders. But there's more to the story. At least, that's what it seems like to me."

"Like what?" he asked.

"Well," she said. "They all seem to march to the beat of this Bill Parker. He's the local big wig. Owns a quarry just outside of town. He's a big fish in this pond. Very powerful, and people fear him. I happened to meet with him this morning, and I can see why."

Howard looked interested.

"You met with him?"

She nodded.

"He invited me to the quarry for a conversation. And I use the term 'invited' loosely."

Howard frowned at this.

"What did he say?"

"He went into detail about a big deal he has on the horizon. Some buyer for his quarry. He expressed his concern that I might disrupt this deal if I were to stick my nose in the wrong place. And then he punctuated his sentiments with a veiled threat."

Howard sat back in his seat.

"What sort of threat?"

Tracy shook her head.

"I wouldn't worry about it. I doubt there's any real bite to his bark. If he's worried about one PI snooping around, the last thing he'll want is an even bigger investigation if something were to happen to me. It's just bullying. But he's definitely got the rest of this town under his thumb, including the sheriff. And I think Parker's son leverages that fear and power to run amok in this place. I think he's a potential suspect in Caroline Duncan's murder."

Howard furrowed his brow.

"This is the young man you got into it with at the bar?"

Tracy nodded.

Howard took a breath and shook his head.

"I need to eat. Are there any good places in town?"

Tracy shook her head.

"No," she said. "I think we'd better order in. It's hard enough trying to get anyone to talk to me as it is. The last thing I need is to be seen with you."

He sighed.

"Alright," he said. "Do they have pizza in this place?"

They spent the next several hours discussing the state's charges against Peter Teller. Howard filled her in on the DA's case, which seemed astonishingly thin. Although the lawyer assured her that he'd seen clients get life sentences based on much, much less.

The state had no murder weapon and no forensics. But they did have witnesses, one of which was the nosy hotel proprietor, who claimed to have heard violent arguments between the couple in the days leading up to the murder. The DA also had text messages, which seemed to confirm that the couple did, in fact, have a fiery relationship, complete with angry exchanges fueled by mutual jealousy, followed by heartfelt reconciliations, and then, more fighting, and so on. They were young, and they seemed to fight the way many young people do. But viewed from the lens of an eventual murder, the conversations did not look good from the boyfriend's perspective or that of his defense attorney.

Eventually, the hours piled up until the sun vanished below the horizon, and then the food was replaced by whiskey as Tracy and Howard put their work aside.

Tracy had secured a bottle from the local liquor store, the one place where the people didn't seem to care whether she was a local or a visitor from the moon.

Howard watched as she filled his glass halfway. Then, he turned and sipped from it slowly, while staring out the window. Outside, the town's street cooled in the absence of the sweltering sun, which colored the edge of the sky with rosy flares of dying light.

"It looks like such a pleasant place," he said. "Like something from a postcard."

Tracy shook her head.

"In this case, looks are very deceiving."

He nodded.

"I'm driving back to Charleston early in the morning. What are your plans here?"

Tracy sipped from her glass and thought for a moment.

"Not sure. It'll come to me. Why don't we take a break from this case and talk about something else?"

He looked at her and raised his eyebrows.

"Like what?"

She thought for a moment.

"How long have you known Jimmy?" she asked.

He thought for a moment.

"Oh, I guess it's been about ten years now. Seems like longer."

She nodded.

"Yeah, I get that."

He chuckled.

"Yeah, he's a bit of a character."

She nodded.

"Got any good stories about him?"

Howard scratched his jaw.

"Honestly, most of my best stories about Jimmy are protected by attorney-client privilege."

She frowned at this.

"But you're not just his lawyer? You guys are friends. Is that right?"

Howard nodded.

"Oh, yeah. I mean, as much as Jimmy has friends, I'd say I'm that much of a friend."

Tracy nodded.

"Yeah."

Howard gave a little smile.

"He's a complicated person. I'm sure you've noticed that. He's not always easy to get along with. But there's nobody you'd rather have on your side in a tough spot. And, at the same time, I wouldn't want to be on his bad side either. So, I try to avoid that as much as possible."

She took a drink from her glass and set it down.

"The chatter surrounding him is that he's connected somehow."

Howard looked puzzled.

"Connected?"

Tracy gave him a doubtful look.

"Yes."

He rubbed his jaw thoughtfully.

"You mean to the mob?"

She shrugged.

"Let's just call it organized crime."

He gave a look of false innocence.

"I wouldn't know anything about that. And if I did, I certainly wouldn't talk about it."

He watched her as she turned away and shook her head.

"Listen," he said. "Jimmy's a good guy. Complicated, yes. But he's a good guy. At least in my book. He and I don't see the world the same, it's true. He's jaded, and his moral compass isn't always pointed north. But he's trustworthy and loyal if he thinks you deserve it."

Tracy picked up her glass.

"Yeah."

He watched her take a drink, his brows furrowed as he considered her for a moment.

"I knew your father," he said.

She swallowed and set her glass back down.

"Is that right?"

He nodded.

"I was sorry to hear about—" He paused for a moment as if searching for the right word. "What occurred."

She raised her brows while she stared down at her glass.

"What occurred," she repeated. "You mean all the criminal misconduct?

He swallowed.

"Yeah. I guess."

She shook her head.

"I'm not the author of his misadventures. Anyway, I'm over it."

She turned to face him.

"Why don't you tell me about yourself a little?"

He smiled.

"What would you like to know?"

She thought for a moment.

"Tell me what it's like to be a criminal defense lawyer."

His smile vanished, and his face hardened as he stared deeply into her eyes.

"I deal with some of the worst people in the world. People who will lie and cheat to get their way. They have no moral reservations about what they do or say." He shrugged. "It's my job as a criminal defense attorney to protect my clients from these people."

Tracy laughed.

"Nice. Is that your trademark answer?"

He nodded.

"I have it locked and loaded at all times."

She nodded.

"Seriously, though. What's it like?"

He scratched his jaw and thought for a moment.

"It has its moments. It's always gratifying winning motions to keep illegally obtained evidence out of court, especially when the cops and the DA have been so arrogant about it. Getting to hear 'not guilty' after a hard-fought trial is also a nice little thrill, especially when the cops and the DA have been so arrogant about it."

He raised his eyebrows.

"Notice a pattern?"

She gave a little smile.

"I understand."

He took a drink from his glass and set it back down.

"Honestly, there's a lot of paperwork. It's not as glamorous as the movies suggest. Every now and then, though, there's a thrilling moment that comes along."

Tracy nodded.

"What's one of your most memorable cases?"

He raised his brows, and his eyes seemed to twinkle.

"One of my favorites happened before I got into criminal law. When I was first getting my feet wet in the profession, I had a guy walk into my office with half an old hamburger. He told me the day before he ordered the item and explicitly said no sesame seeds. Said he mentioned that he was deathly allergic to them and that he would get anaphylaxis if exposed. Now, why anyone with that kind of allergy would even risk eating at a burger joint is beyond me. But this guy did, and he was assured that there would be no sesame seeds on the bun.

"When his order came up, the guy was assured that the burger had no sesame seeds. And the bun did look like it had no seeds, according to him. But about an hour or two later, after having his stomach pumped at the ER, he learned from the attending doctor that he had ingested at least three sesame seeds.

"So, the guy goes back to the restaurant, and the manager offers him 100 bucks and some coupons. He gets mad and drives straight to my office. I listen to the guy's story and immediately pick up the phone. I call the store manager, who connects me to the owner, who eventually connects me with his lawyer. I explain the situation and offer to settle for 20 grand. I stress that the claim will be worth far more in front of a jury and tell him we had two witnesses that heard the guy very clearly mention he was allergic and could die if he ate sesame seeds."

He looked at her and gave a little smile.

"Long story short, I had a $20,000 check delivered by courier to my office by the end of the week. I ended up with $7,000 of the money and never even got up from my desk."

Tracy frowned.

"That's not the kind of story I had in mind."

Howard laughed.

"Well, it's memorable to me."

She took a drink and nodded.

"Fair enough. How about instead, you tell me the craziest criminal case you've ever brought to trial."

Howard raised his eyebrows.

"My craziest criminal cases never really go to trial because they are too crazy. Juries are unpredictable enough with non-crazy cases. So, the prosecutors are usually more inclined to plea bargain."

She nodded.

"Ok. How about your most memorable criminal case?"

"That's easy. I defended a client accused of killing someone while performing a crush fetish."

Tracy furrowed her brows.

"A what?

Howard nodded.

"That's what I said when I first heard it too. It seems there are people out there that get off on seeing things get crushed or being crushed themselves. Enough people, in fact, that there's a whole online community about it."

Tracy looked at him as if he'd spoken Latin.

"What?"

Howard looked amused.

"So, as I understand it," he said, "the fetish is associated with a subcategory of paraphilias, which are atypical sexual interests. Specifically, a crush fetish involves deriving sexual arousal from watching objects, insects or sometimes even small animals being crushed. And as the fetish progresses, the person often desires to be the one that gets crushed."

Tracy pinched her eyebrows together.

"What?"

Howard laughed.

"I'm serious. It was explained to me that crush fetishes fall under the broader category of macrophilia, which is a fetish involving domination, often with an emphasis on the contrast between the small and large. In other words, a big woman lying on top of a man until he can't breathe. Apparently, when the person's chest is compressed enough, oxygen is deprived, and a person gets a high, which contributes to a more intense orgasm."

Tracy stared at him and shook her head.

"You're making this up."

Howard shook his head.

"Absolutely not. My client was 400 pounds at least. She lay on her boyfriend until he suffocated. The DA charged her with murder. Absolutely refused to plea down the charges. We went to court, and I put up a strong case that the two were in love. The jury agreed, and she got off."

Tracy shook her head.

"Did she do it on purpose?"

He frowned.

"I don't know. She may have. They certainly had a history of domestic violence."

Tracy furrowed her brows.

"It doesn't bother you that you may have helped a guilty person go free?"

Howard shook his head.

"The role of a defense attorney is to make damn sure their client's rights are protected and that the government plays by the rules. Even the most violent, disturbing crimes have to be proven beyond a reasonable doubt and in accordance with the rules that govern our judicial system. My job is to make sure the state can prove that every single bit of evidence was properly collected, stored and processed. And then confirm that this same evidence is even relevant to the case. If the government does its job the way it's supposed to and my client is actually guilty, I should never have a chance to win. My job is to make sure the government does its job."

She raised her eyebrows.

"Sounds like I touched a nerve."

He shook his head.

"No. Not really," he said. "It's just that it has always confused me. People ask lawyers how they can live with the idea of defending someone who might be guilty of a crime. But no one ever asks a doctor how they can live with the idea of providing medical care to a criminal. Both do it the same way: professionally and without ridiculous sanctimony."

She shook her head.

"But if you know the client is guilty of murder, it has to bother you on some level."

He shook his head.

"Clients don't typically come out and say "I'm guilty. Get me off." Most of the time, they profess their innocence, and I have to proceed on the assumption that they are being truthful. On occasion, they may admit their guilt and ask me to help them get the best deal. If someone were to actually come right out and admit guilt and ask me to help them get away with the crime, I would decline the case because I will not fabricate a case, nor will I allow witnesses to get on the stand and testify to things I know to be untrue."

Tracy pursed her lips and nodded.

"But what if you know in your heart that they are lying to you about their innocence?"

He shook his head.

"You can't ever really know. But if I do suspect their guilt, and the evidence against them is strong, I will advise that the client take a plea deal if one becomes available. Sometimes that's not possible because the nature of the charge means an extremely long sentence. Sometimes, the client is simply averse to the notion of any plea agreement. In that case, if the client insists on a trial, they are entitled to it. And I have no choice but to give my best effort because it's my ethical and constitutional duty. Even if the case is indefensible, you just have to do the best you can with whatever facts you have. You make sure the state follows the rules. You object when you can. You hope at least one juror doubts the prosecution and forces a mistrial."

She shook her head.

"You go to court even if you know you can't win?"

He shook his head.

"There are varying degrees of winning. Some of my proudest moments are minor victories. Establishing weaknesses in the prosecution's case, so a client gets five years instead of a life sentence. Getting a murder charge reduced to manslaughter. Attacking prior convictions in a "three-strikes" case. The client still goes to jail, but I did my best to make the punishment fair and equitable."

Tracy took and drink and thought about his words.

"I don't know," she said. "I get what you're saying, but I just don't think I could sleep at night defending someone that I know committed rape or murder or child abuse."

He frowned at her.

"I get more sleep defending the guilty than I do the innocent."

She furrowed her brows.

"Explain."

He took a breath and frowned.

"Representing a guilty client is straightforward. The government has the burden of proof. If I can't argue self-defense, I simply focus on holding the government to its proof by questioning evidence, impeaching its witnesses and arguing against the prosecution's inferences. With an innocent client, I still have to do all of that, but the burden of proof shifts to me. And it's a lot easier to prove that something happened than to prove that something didn't."

He frowned at her.

"The State has amazing resources," he continued. "With one case, they can commit dozens and dozens of cops and detectives, forensic analysts, psychiatric professionals. Expert after expert. And all with no budget constraints. Very few defendants have the resources to match the state."

He looked at her and shook his head slowly.

"When a lawyer knows their client is not guilty, the case can consume them, especially if they face the death penalty or a life sentence. It trumps everything. Social engagements, golf, dinners, sleep. You think about it constantly because you know a conviction means you get to spend the rest of your life wondering if you could have changed the outcome by doing a little bit more. Just a few more hours examining documents. Bringing on a different witness. The case can gnaw at your mind for years. It can change you in deeply personal ways."

She looked at him and sighed.

"Do you think that's what you have right now with this case?"

He stared back at her and raised his eyebrows.

"You tell me."

She took in a deep breath and picked up her glass. He watched while she took a big drink. She set the glass back down and frowned at it.

"Yes," she said. "But I've been wrong before."

Chapter 7

The next morning, Tracy awoke with a pounding head and a parched mouth. Howard had said goodnight and left for his room before ten. But she continued to drink alone for another hour at least. And now she cursed herself as she stumbled out of bed and staggered to the bathroom.

The light stung her eyes as she flipped the switch, and a frazzled-looking woman stared back from the other side of the mirror, her red-rimmed eyes filled with harsh judgments. Tracy sighed and approached the sink. She turned the handle and released a cold pillar of water. She bent and drank until her belly was full. Then, she stood up and listened as the phone rang in the other room.

Without hurrying, she turned off the faucet and gave her chaotic hair one last look. Then, she turned and made her way toward the ringing.

"Hello," she said as she put the receiver to her ear.

"Ms. Sterling," said the hotel proprietor, her voice heavily accented and sickeningly sweet.

"Yes."

"There's a gentleman waiting for you in the lobby."

Tracy rubbed her forehead.

"Who is it?"

The proprietor was quiet for a moment.

"I believe it is the brother of Caroline Duncan," she said at last.

Tracy perked up a little.

"Ok. I'll be down in a moment."

She hung up the phone and hurried to the bathroom. With a quick hand, she did her best to tame the riot of tangled her and applied enough makeup to make herself look human. Then, she threw on some clothes and went downstairs.

She found the young man waiting for her in the hotel lobby. Sitting alone on the little sofa, he appeared just as disheveled as he had the previous day. He held no phone. And he read no magazine. He just sat alone, his body completely still as he stared forward at the wall in an autistic sort of way that made Tracy furrow her brow as she approached him from the side.

"Hello, Carter."

He turned and looked up at her, his deep brown eyes appearing almost solid pupil as they stared out from under his low black bangs. He appeared to be wearing the same shirt from the day before, and his black hair glistened with oil beneath the lobby lights. He smelled of marijuana, and Tracy glanced up at the hotel proprietor, who was trying to look busy behind the counter several feet away.

"Hello," said Carter as he looked at her with hazy eyes and a pale blank face.

Tracy gave him a friendly smile.

"Do you have some information for me?"

He looked around.

"Not here."

She nodded.

"I agree. What do you have in mind?"

"There's a place down the road," he said.

He stood and led her out of the hotel, while the woman behind the counter watched them from the edge of her eye. Outside, the early afternoon air was stifling, and Tracy felt her shirt stick to her back as sweat began to leak from her pores.

While the two of them walked, people flicked curious glances. their faces pinching with private thoughts as they moved about the downtown sidewalks. And what an odd pair Tracy and the young man must have made. Though, she doubted odd pairings were required to catch the attention of the nosy people in this strange and unsettling place.

Carter led her down the street until they arrived at a small pizza parlor. Inside, the place was mostly empty, save for a middle-aged man behind the counter and a pair of young children playing a video game in one far corner. Carter waved at the employee as they entered, and the man gave him a friendly nod.

"Can I get you folks somethin?"

Carter shook his head.

"No, thanks. We're just going to talk a bit if that's ok."

The man nodded and picked up a broom.

"Fine by me."

He slipped a pair of headphones over his ears and started sweeping the floor.

"This place is quiet," said Carter as he looked back over his shoulder. "I come here a lot."

Tracy nodded as they approached a booth and sat.

"It looks fine," she said. "So, what have you got for me?"

He looked at her.

"I heard you met Beaux Parker last night."

She nodded.

"Unfortunately, yes. And his father this morning."

He nodded.

"So, you're getting the picture, I take it."

She nodded.

"Yes."

He took in a breath as he looked at her. His bold eyes seemed to hold contact with hers at all times, and there was no perceivable reticence in the way he appraised her.

"What's New York like?" he asked.

"What?"

He shrugged.

"I'd like to go."

"It's unique," she said. "I'll tell you all about it after we discuss your sister."

He nodded.

"Ok."

She raised her eyebrows.

"Can you start by telling me what happened the night of her death?"

He nodded.

"I was in my room listening to music. My mom said Caroline was leaving in the morning. But she was on her way to say goodbye. She never showed up. After a while, my mom called the sheriff."

Tracy nodded.

"And then what happened?"

He shook his head.

"We didn't hear anything until dawn. That's when the sheriff showed up and told us what happened."

Tracy frowned.

"Did he say anything else? Did he question you?"

He nodded.

"Not really. He told us she had been killed. And when my mom stopped crying, he told us they already had her boyfriend in custody."

"That's it?" asked Tracy.

He nodded.

"That's all I know. My mom might know more, but she's probably a dead end."

Tracy nodded and looked over at the two boys playing the video game.

"I tried to talk to Caroline's friend, Maddie Taylor," she said as she turned her eyes back on Carter. "This was before we were interrupted by Beaux Parker. She seemed hesitant. Like someone told her not to talk to me."

He nodded.

"That sounds about right."

"Do you think someone told her to keep her mouth shut?"

He looked at her with his dark, probing eyes.

"I doubt she needed to be told."

Tracy sat back and looked at him.

"I'm assuming she felt threatened by the Parker family, am I correct?"

He nodded.

"Yes."

"Do you think they're involved in your sister's murder?"

He shook his head.

"I don't know."

Tracy frowned at him.

"First, I can't get Maddie Taylor to talk to me. Next, I'm accosted by Beaux Parker. Then, yesterday, in a roundabout way, his

63

father suggested I might be in danger if I don't wrap up my investigation and leave town. Don't you find that strange?"

He shook his head.

"Not really."

She furrowed her brows.

"Why not?"

"Because it's always been like that here. It's why Caroline left in the first place. It's why I want to leave. This place has always been under the Parker family's thumb. No one wants to piss them off. And no one is exactly sure what will piss them off next because everything seems to do the job. People just try to err on the side of caution, I think. And that usually starts with not talking to outsiders."

Tracy glanced over at the man behind the counter, but he was listening to his headphones as he swept the floor.

"Listen, Carter. I need your help. Can you tell me where Maddie Taylor lives? I need to talk to her."

He nodded.

"Yes. But I don't think she will talk to you."

Tracy nodded.

"I understand. But I need to try."

He nodded.

"It's out in the boondocks about five miles outside of town. I'll draw you a map."

She waited while he scribbled on the back of a paper menu. Then, she took the paper and slipped it into her pocket.

"I appreciate it," she said. "Now, is there anything else you can tell me?"

He tilted his head slightly.

"Like what?"

"Did your sister have any enemies from her high school days? Can you think of anyone who might want to harm her?"

He shook his head.

"Not really. But she's older. And we didn't run in the same circles. So, I can't be sure."

"What about potential witnesses? Is there a chance someone might have seen the crime?"

He shook his head.

"The only people who live out there are me and my mom. The closest other person is Silas Brown, but his house is at least a mile from the pond."

Tracy leaned down and wrote the name down.

"And who is this?"

"He's just an old man who lives by himself out in the deep woods. A hermit, I guess. He was in the war. I don't know which war. One of the old ones. Anyway, he's touched, so everyone knows to stay off his land."

Tracy furrowed her brows.

"Touched?"

"Crazy," said Carter.

Tracy nodded.

"Ah," she said. "I see. Well, that's an interesting lead."

He shook his head.

"I doubt it. He's basically a ghost that keeps to himself. And I don't even know if he's still out there. Anyway, he's got to be a hundred at least. If he's still alive."

Tracy nodded.

"Well, let's see what Maddie Taylor knows. And I'll go from there."

He looked at her with those dark, piercing eyes.

"You're going out there today?"

She nodded.

"Right after I get finished here."

About an hour later, Tracy drove alone down the deserted backroads outside of town. All around her, the road was lined with towering live oaks and bald cypresses, which swayed like waving giants amid the hot summer breeze. As she pushed out into the dense, unpopulated hinterlands, her tires threw clouds of dust high and wide into the air while the shocks jostled and squealed along the bad dirt road.

Tracy grimaced as the vehicle bounced violently against a deep hole carved out by years of hard weather. She cursed and slowed a bit as the scenery whizzed by outside the window.

Out in the road, a pair of buzzards pulled strings of leathered flesh from a dead rabbit. She curled her lip and slowed long enough for their great flapping wings to carry them up and into the wind. Then, she watched in her rearview mirror as they dropped slowly back down to their meal and started tearing at the rotting flesh with their gnarled beaks.

After a while, she pulled over to the side of the road. Her phone had lost service two miles back, and without GPS, she was reduced to deciphering the chicken scratch Carter had scribbled onto a piece of paper.

She held the paper up and squinted at it. She turned it sideways and shook her head.

"Great," she hissed as she pulled back out onto the road.

The tires spun a little on the loose dirt before they finally bit. And then, she saw a glint of metal in her rearview mirror. She frowned at the approaching vehicle as she picked up speed. It was coming up fast behind her. And a big cloud of dirt billowed up in its wake.

She watched as the vehicle grew closer. It was a new bright red Dodge pickup truck with an engine that gobbled up the road in great productive bites. Tracy narrowed her eyes as it took on size in the reflective glass.

Soon, the thing came roaring up on Tracy's rear bumper, its horn blaring like a freight train without a single pause. Tracy flinched a little in preparation for an impact, but just before it closed, the truck let itself fall back several feet without ceasing the incessant honking.

The old road wasn't quite two lanes. And the pickup driver dodged and weaved side to side, trying to force Tracy to move aside and give it room to pass. She pushed down on the accelerator. The sound of knocks and clicks filled her car as bits of rock and dirt clods pinged up from underneath. Her heart tapped against her chest as the truck let itself fall back a few yards. Then, it roared forward again with great speed.

Now, the driver flashed his headlights. And for a moment, Tracy considered pulling over. All the while, her eyes darted from the road to her rearview mirror, as she tried to get a look at the driver, whose face lay concealed behind the bright glint of the reflected afternoon sun.

A flat stretch of shoulder manifested just ahead to the left, and the pickup seized its chance. As both vehicles neared the stretch, the driver mashed the gas, and his engine rumbled like a crack of thunder as the vehicle dipped into the rough grassy shoulder and easily made it around Tracy and back onto the road.

As the truck passed, Tracy caught a glimpse of the driver. It was Beaux Parker, and he had a friend beside him in the passenger seat. Another rode in the back of the truck. And this young man sneered at Tracy as the pickup moved in front of her and immediately slammed on its brakes.

Tracy gripped the steering wheel and tapped the brakes until her car closed up tight on the truck's rear bumper. Then, the pickup raced forward, while the young man grinned at her from his perch in the bed of the truck.

Tracy cursed and drove forward slowly, the truck altering its speed to stay a few yards in front of her. And then, she saw a thick, muscled arm drape out the driver's side window. Her eyes traveled to the hand, which held a half-empty 40-ounce bottle of beer.

Before she could veer, the arm pitched the bottle several feet into the air. It seemed to pause for a moment, suspended in the sky as it drifted end over end. And then, it descended flush on the hood of Tracy's car, exploding against it with the percussion of a tiny bomb.

Tracy slammed on her brakes and skidded to a halt, her car vanishing amid a cloud of dust as glass and beer clacked and splattered against her windshield. She coughed as the dust and dirt flooded into her open windows. Then, she heard the sound of the truck backing up. Doors opened and closed. And she could hear the sound of heavy boots crunching against gravel outside.

Without thinking, Tracy opened her car door and stepped outside. The dusty haze was starting to clear, and out of it, Beaux and his two friends approached, their cruel faces split with wide grins as they stopped in the road and stood.

"I told you I'd be seeing you again," said Bill Parker's son as he held his hands out to his side. "We've got some unfinished business."

Tracy looked at each of the young men as she stepped away from her car.

"You're a fucking idiot," she said. "You could have killed someone."

Beaux's grin vanished, and he seemed to swell in size.

"Nobody talks to me like that."

He looked at one of his friends and gave him a nod. Tracy watched as the young man turned and walked back to the pickup truck. As Beaux glared at her, his friend retrieved a heavy tire iron from the bed of the truck. Tracy lowered her eyebrows as the man returned and placed the tool in Beaux's hand. His grin returned as he dropped the long hunk of metal to his side.

"Time to pay the piper," he said.

Tracy watched as the other two men spread apart just as they had done the other night outside the bar. Each one took a position on her right and left flanks, while Beaux tapped the tire iron against an empty palm.

"You sure you want to go this route?" asked Tracy.

The young man grinned and took a step forward. And then, he stopped as Tracy withdrew her pistol. With a bored expression, she held the gun out to her side and sighed.

"We done here?" she asked.

The other men had flinched a little at the sight of the weapon, but Beaux merely regarded it with a doubtful glare.

"You're not gonna shoot me."

He took another step forward, and Tracy raised the gun. Without speaking, she popped off a couple of shots at the road just inches before Beaux's feet. Dust floated up in cloudy wisps, as birds fled the trees in response to the booming commotion. Beaux's friends put their hands up and retreated back to their leader.

"Now, are we done?" asked Tracy.

Beaux stared at her, his eyes throwing out hate. He raised the tire iron with his big arm and held it out as if it were the weight of a small stick. He pointed it at her and flashed his teeth.

"This ain't over. As soon as you get back in that car, I'm gonna run you into a ditch."

Tracy thought for a moment and looked past them. While they watched, she leveled her pistol at his truck and pulled the trigger. The shot echoed off the trees. And then there came a low, whiny hiss as one of the truck's tires deflated.

Beaux turned and started to yell, but his words were drowned away by another shot and a second gush of air as another tire went flat.

The three young men stared at the vehicle with their jaws agape, as if they had just stood witness to some implausible magic that cast their reality in a new light.

Tracy took a breath and holstered her pistol.

"You fellas have a great rest of your day."

The three men turned and watched mutely as she got in her car and drove back to town.

Chapter 8

When Tracy arrived at the hotel, the sheriff was waiting for her in the lobby. He stood up from one of the sofas and looked at her, his hat in his hand, as he regarded her with an apologetic frown.

"I'm afraid I'm gonna have to take you in, Ms. Sterling."

She glanced over at the hotel proprietor, who was pretending not to listen while she wiped down the counter.

"What?" asked Tracy as she looked back at the sheriff.

He pursed his lips.

"Got a complaint from Bill Parker. Said you was harassing his son and his friends."

Tracy shook her head.

"Come on, Sheriff, you know that's not what happened. They were harassing me."

He shrugged.

"Did you shoot his tires out?"

She started to speak, but he held his hand up.

"I'm sorry," he said as he put his hat on. "I gotta take you in."

He approached, and she shook her head.

"I had no choice. It was the only way to keep them off me."

He sighed.

"You coulda called me."

She forced a laugh, and his face darkened.

"You got a piece on you?"

She reached inside her jacket and pulled the pistol from its holster. She handed it to him, and he looked it over.

"I'm sorry," he said as he slipped it into his belt. "But the law's the law."

"Is it?" she asked as she glared at him.

He frowned at her and took her by the arm. Tracy glared at the hotel proprietor, who averted her eyes and walked away from the counter.

"What?" said Tracy. "No cuffs?"

The sheriff sighed.

"Come on, now," he said as he led her out of the hotel. "Let's keep this civil."

An hour later, she stood in a small jail cell next to a soiled cot and a single toilet with a dark ring at the bottom of the bowl. The place smelled of mildew and sweat, and the air hung heavy and hot, as she withstrained a gag with every breath. In the other room, the sheriff sat at his desk, his cowboy boots up on the desk as he leaned back in his chair, chatting with someone on the phone. She walked over to the bars and pressed against them. She hung her arms out and let the cool metal touch her warm, sticky skin.

At last, the sheriff hung up the phone and got to his feet. He approached with a ring of keys and gave her that same apologetic frown.

"That was your lawyer friend on the phone," he said.

Tracy shook her head.

"Great."

The sheriff held out the ring of keys, and they jangled together. He squinted his eyes and went through them until he found the right one. Then, he jammed it into the slot and gave it a twist. The door squealed as he pulled it open.

"Come on over and have a chat with me," he said.

Tracy stepped out of the stinking cell and followed him to his desk. There was a little plastic chair positioned before it, and it squeaked as she sat.

"Your lawyer friend said he'd pay your bail," he said as he sat back down behind his desk. "But I told him it weren't necessary if you were to be on your way."

Tracy's eyes flicked up.

"What about Beaux Parker?" she asked.

The sheriff sucked his cheek for a moment as he looked at her.

70

"His daddy will agree to drop the charges if you move on."

She shook her head slowly, her eyes regarding the sheriff with contempt.

"What the hell is going on in this place?" she asked. "This Bill Parker seems to have a hold on everyone. And you seem content to sit back and let it happen."

The sheriff glared at her.

"I don't know what you're talking about," he said. "What I do know is you committed a serious crime. A crime that comes with jail time around here. And you're being given a lifeline that you should take while you still can."

She sat back and folded her arms.

"I was paid to do a job."

The sheriff shook his head.

"Not no more. Your lawyer friend says your job is over, and he'll take things from here. You're to head back to the airport and fly on home to New York."

He looked at her and turned his hand over.

"There it is," he said.

She sat back in her seat. She watched a fly scuttle across the sheriff's desk.

"Listen," said the sheriff as he leaned forward and folded his hands atop his desk. "It's better this way. You just don't know it. I admire your tenacity. I truly do. But you're runnin up against some powerful folk. People who don't want their business disrupted."

She looked up at him.

"Like Bill Parker, you mean."

The sheriff shrugged.

"It is what it is. Anyway, you're wasting your time. That Caroline girl was killed by her boyfriend, and the DA will prove it in a court of law. There ain't nothin out here that's gonna change that. You're just pissin in people's cornflakes. And there ain't no reason for it."

Tracy cocked her head a little.

"Bill Parker sure is lucky to have a guy like you as sheriff."

He looked at her, but he didn't seem angered. Instead, he only sat back and shook his head.

"That's fine," he said. "You can say what you like as long as you go on home."

She stood up and looked down at him.

71

"I'll take my gun."

He shook his head.

"No. I'm afraid I'm gonna have to hold onto it."

She lowered her eyebrows.

"Why?"

"It's evidence in a crime," he said.

She put a hand on her hip.

"I thought you said the charges were dropped."

He shook his head.

"Not until you're on a plane for New York. I'll FedEx it to you."

She started to argue, but he silenced her with his hand.

"This ain't no negotiation. Now, get on out of here before I change my mind."

She gave him one last look, her eyes traveling up and down his body as her lip curled slightly in disgust. Then, she turned and walked out the door.

Outside, the harsh midday sun hung small and bright in the cloudless blue sky. The street sweltered while people popped in and out of the shade as they moved about their business like kitchen insects hurrying to escape the light. Tracy shook her head as she walked up the street back toward the hotel, her mind cursing the sheriff as she ran a hand over the void where her pistol used to be. It was an uncomfortable, naked sensation that filled her with rage and dread as she felt the eyes of curious people glance in her direction with every other step.

An hour later, she was driving back toward Maddie Taylor's house. This time, she'd been extra careful, pausing here and there to ensure that no one had followed her out of town. And now, as civilization released her to the uncultivated country, she felt a sense of relief amid the quiet solitude, where no one studied her with inquisitive eyes.

As the soaring oaks and cypresses whirred by, she stole glances at the map Carter had drawn for her. Maddie Taylor lived in a modest little house she'd inherited from her mother. The place was about twenty minutes outside of town on the other side of the railroad tracks, and when Tracy saw the iron lines in the coming distance, she knew she was close.

She neared the old railway crossing and slowed. The battered wooden sign bore the stark, black symbol of the railway like a weathered tattoo. There were no crossing safety gates. Just an old post with a pair of red warning lights that looked about as reliable as a two-legged stool. So, Tracy stopped and looked both ways. In each direction, the rusted tracks disappeared into the murky horizon as they stitched their way across the wild country.

When she was satisfied, she crossed over the tracks with a rough thump and made her way up the road. Soon, she popped out of the dense woods into a stretch of open land, where yellow fields sprawled out on either side of the road beneath the lazy afternoon sun. Neat fences lined both sides of the path, their straight pickets overrun by wild tangles of ivy.

Minutes later, she spotted the house sitting alone at the edge of a great tree line. Though old, it was well cared for, its newly painted exterior gleaming white in the sun. Tracy stopped at a little red mailbox and turned up the neat gravel path.

She slowed and parked behind a single car in the driveway. Then, she stepped out amid the afternoon heat, where a symphony of grasshoppers and distant cicadas seeded the air with a steady symphony of whirs and clicks, which rose and fell like a tide.

She shut her door and looked up at the little house. A lonely pink flower stuck up from a ceramic pot on the porch, where an old rocking chair moved slightly in the warm breeze. To the left of the porch, near what looked like the kitchen, she caught a fleeting glimpse of a figure behind a closed curtain. She started toward the house but paused at the shrieking sound of a screen door, which opened to reveal Maddie Taylor, who stepped out onto the porch and put her hands on her hips.

"You was supposed to be here yesterday."

Tracy nodded.

"Yes," she said. "I'm sorry. I ran into some trouble."

The young woman looked her over and frowned.

"What sort of trouble?"

Tracy smiled.

"Nothing important. Can we talk?"

Maddie folded her arms and took in a deep breath.

"I don't want no trouble."

Tracy nodded.

"I don't want to cause you any trouble."

The young woman turned her head and looked off down the empty road. Tracy took a few steps forward, her movements slow, as if she were approaching a feral cat.

"Listen, Maddie. I understand you don't feel comfortable talking to me. I know you're worried about potential repercussions."

`Maddie's eyes flicked over to Tracy's face, and she swallowed.

"But, listen," Tracy continued. "You have nothing to worry about because I'm not going to tell anyone that we talked. I will protect your interests."

The young woman shook her head.

"I don't know. I want to help. I do. I loved Caroline. But you don't know these people."

Tracy pinched her brows together and looked into the young woman's ordinary blue eyes.

"I understand," she said. "Believe me. This is not the first time I've questioned someone who has been worried about blowback from other parties. I've talked to witnesses who were worried about reprisals from the mafia. I know how to keep a secret, Maddie. I just need to know a few things to help point me in the right direction. If you don't feel comfortable answering some of my questions, I will not press the issue."

The young woman looked down at the ground and sighed.

"Ok," she said. "But you'd better come in off the porch."

She turned and opened the screen door, which whined and screeched a little in its old hinges. Tracy followed her across the entryway and into a modest little living room that smelled like moth balls. There were family photos on the walls and a little couch with worn armrests. A big television roared from the far corner of the room. And in front of it, an old man sat in a rocking chair, his leathery brows bunched up as his lips moved with endless silent words.

"Grandpa!" shouted Maddie as they entered the room. "Turn that down."

The old man turned and squinted at her. His face was lined with too many wrinkles to count, and one of his eyes was white with a milky cataractous lens.

"What's that?" he shouted.

"Turn it down!"

He frowned and started tapping the remote control

"That's my granddad," said Maddie. "He's half deaf."

The old man turned and glared at her with his disturbing mismatched eyes.

"I ain't deaf."

"I said you was half deaf," shouted Maddie.

"Oh," said the man as he turned back toward the TV.

"Have a seat," said Maddie as she gestured to an unstable-looking recliner.

Tracy carefully sat and watched as Maddie took a seat on the couch. As if drawn by some sort of unseen gravity, the old man's head turned toward her.

"Who's that?" he asked.

"She's here to talk about Caroline," said Maddie.

"Who?"

"Caroline."

The old man pondered this for a moment.

"That ain't Caroline."

"Hush up and let us talk," said Maddie. She shook her head and looked at Tracy. "I'm sorry. He's an old fool."

Tracy smiled politely.

"It's quite alright. You two live by yourselves out here?"

The young woman nodded.

"My parents died when I was young. Granddad and Grandma raised me. She passed a couple of years ago. So, I'm takin care of him. And believe you me, it's a full-time job."

Tracy nodded.

"That's very good of you."

She shrugged.

"It is what it is. Now, what do you want to know about Caroline?"

With a practiced technique, Tracy began to ask questions, her words carefully chosen as she probed at the young woman's defenses. At first, the details came slowly. But after a while, the logjam seemed to break apart, and the words began to float freely, like trapped birds escaping from the tiny door of an open cage.

Once the floodgates fell, the waters came gushing forth like a river, and Tracy nodded politely as she jotted down notes on a legal pad. Most of Maddie's words were little more than useless small-town gossip. And Tracy felt very much like a therapist nodding along to the rantings of a stifled small-town soul.

At last, the young woman took a breath, and Tracy set her pen down.

"What can you tell me about Beaux Parker?" she asked.

Maddie stiffened in her seat, and Tracy thought she might have seen the old man's jaw flex beneath his sagging skin.

"I don't wanna talk about him, if that's alright."

Tracy looked over at the old man, who seemed to give an approving nod.

"Alright," said Tracy. "Can you at least tell me if he and Caroline ever had any run-ins? Did he have any animosity against her? Any reason to dislike her?"

Maddie shook her head.

"He's had run-ins with just about everybody in this town. He was a bully in school. And he's still a bully. I'm sure Caroline had reason to hate him, but everybody does."

Tracy nodded.

"Ok," she said. "What about Caroline's brother?"

Maddie raised her eyebrows.

"Carter?" she said. "He's weird. Gross, I guess. But most of the boys in this town are. Caroline never had much time for him. They weren't that close."

Tracy nodded.

"What do you mean weird?"

She furrowed her brows and thought for a moment.

"I don't know. Just creepy, I guess. We'd catch him lookin at our bodies when we went over to their house. But I guess that ain't super weird if you think about it. I don't know. He's just weird. Have you met him?"

Tracy nodded.

"I think he's on drugs or somethin," Maddie continued. "That would explain a lot. If he ain't, then he's definitely got somethin wrong with him, cause normal folk don't act that way."

Tracy nodded and sat back in her chair.

"You said he and Caroline weren't close. Was there animosity between them?"

Maddie shook her head.

"No more than any other brother and sister, I guess. Caroline wasn't close to him or her mama. She hated this place and everyone in it. Except for me. Anyway, she wanted out."

Tracy nodded.

76

"What do you know about Silas Brown?"

Maddie shrugged.

"He's just some crazy old coot that lives out yonder in no man's land. I mean, I should probably say he used to. I don't know if he does no more. Ain't nobody seen him in a long time. He may have died for all I know. You want some tea?"

Tracy looked at her for a moment and then forced a polite smile.

"Sure."

Maddie stood up and walked into the kitchen. Tracy watched her leave the room and then bent over her notepad to jot down some thoughts.

"He was in Vietnam," said the old man.

Tracy looked up with surprise, as if a corpse had lifted from its coffin to speak.

"I'm sorry?"

The old man turned his ghostly gaze on her.

"Silas Brown. He was in Vietnam."

"Is that right?" asked Tracy.

The old man nodded.

"It fucked up his brain. He come back all strange. Wouldn't talk to nobody. Kept to himself out at his family's old place. Out in those deep woods , where even I don't like to go in. The low, low country. His family been out there for generations. They all gone now. But he's still out there. If'n he's still alive. Which he may not be no more."

The old man pushed his lower lip out thoughtfully.

"I didn't serve in the war on account of my foot," he continued as he looked down at his leg. Tracy followed his eyes to what looked like half a foot.

"My goodness," she said.

He nodded.

"I lost it when I was a boy. Me and my cousin was tryin to chop wood into vertical slices. He missed, and the blade kinda bounced off the log and found its way into my foot. I bout bled out right there. But I didn't. Instead, I got this foot."

Tracy frowned.

"I'm very sorry."

He shrugged.

"I ain't. It kept me out the war."

77

Maddie returned with tea, her head shaking as she entered the room.

"Are you talking about your foot again, Grandpa?"

He looked at the television and sucked at his cheek.

"So, what if I am?"

She shook her head as she handed Tracy her tea.

"It's either the fuckin foot or goddamn politics," she said.

The old man looked at them both.

"The world's headed to hell in a handbasket. And I ain't afraid to say it."

Tracy gave a polite smile as Maddie sat back down on the couch.

"Sir," Tracy said, "Before, you said Silas Brown came back strange after the war. Can you tell me more about that?"

Maddie flashed a look at her grandfather.

"Oh, not this again." She turned toward Tracy. "I've been hearing this all my life."

The old man's weathered face soured, and he looked away.

"Hearing about what exactly?" asked Tracy.

Maddie shook her head and sighed.

"Silas Brown is like the boogieman around here. Every parent tells their kids not to go near his land. I still remember the stories the other kids would tell in the schoolyard. That he was a pedophile who liked to diddle little boys. That he trapped kids like animals and ate their skin. None of it's true. It's all just a bunch of small-town bullshit. Hell, I've never even laid eyes on Silas Brown. For all I know, he doesn't even really exist."

The old man turned and raised his eyebrows.

"Oh, he exists. You'd better damn well believe it."

Tracy furrowed her brow.

"Did you know him personally?"

The old man shook his head.

"He's ten years older than me. So, we didn't exactly fraternize with the same folk. I was still playin with toy cars when he went off to the war. But I do know that my daddy said he was a dangerous man with a broken mind. And my daddy never told a lie in his life."

Maddie shook her head.

"Ten years older than you, and he's dangerous." She gestured toward her grandfather. "You cain't even walk to the bathroom without help."

Tracy looked at Maddie.

"Do you think this man could have been responsible for Caroline's death?"

"Absolutely," interrupted the old man.

"Grandpa!" hissed Maddie. She looked at Tracy. "If Silas Brown is still alive, he's gotta be 90, at least. Caroline was one of the most athletic girls at our high school. She ran track, and she played on the basketball team. She could run all day. Even with the boys. I can't envision no 90-year-old man holdin her head underwater."

Tracy nodded.

"Fair enough," she said. "But I'd still like to talk to him."

The old man looked at her, and the skin around his eyes stretched wide, the milky cataract seeming to bore into her very soul.

"Don't you ever even think about going onto that man's land," he said. "He kill you just as soon as look at you. Then, he might even eat you in the bargain."

Maddie shook her head.

"You see what I mean?"

Tracy gave a polite smile to the old man.

"I'll be careful."

He shook his head and turned back toward the television.

"Young folk think they know everything. They got to touch the stove to make sure it's really hot. It don't do no good to tell em it's hot. They got to touch it to see for theyselves."

He shook his head, while Maddie sighed.

"It wouldn't do you no good anyways," said the young woman. "Even if he is alive out there, he's crazy as all hell. Senile probably too. He couldn't even tell you what year it was, would be my guess. Anyways, you do what you want. Just so long as you leave our names out of it. I got enough problems tryin to make ends meet and take care of this old coot. I don't need the Parker boys in my business. I leave them alone and hope they do the same to me."

Tracy nodded.

"Understood. If it comes up, I'll tell anyone who asks that I tried to talk to you, and you sent me away."

Maddie gave her a smile.

"Thank you," she said. "I'd tell you more if I could. But I honestly don't know that much. Me and Caroline were close when she lived here. We kind of drifted apart a little when she went to college. It was good to see her and all. But things felt different, especially with her new boyfriend."

Tracy nodded.

"Before I go, can you tell me your impressions of her boyfriend?"

Maddie thought for a moment.

"He was nice enough. Kind of quiet. But who wouldn't be if they found themselves a stranger in a place like this??

Tracy nodded.

"Did they get in any fights that you saw? Any arguments?"

She thought for a moment.

"A little, I guess. Nothin crazy. Nothin like me and my boyfriend, I'll tell you that. We get to fightin, and the birds fly out the trees."

Tracy nodded.

"Ok," she said. "Well, I won't take any more of your time. If you think of anything else, give me a call."

She handed Maddie a card and stood. She smiled and said her goodbyes. Then, she turned and made her way outside, where the sun had begun its descent toward the trees-speckled horizon. She stood on the porch and looked at the iron-red clouds, which burned like vivid plumes at the edge of the world. The rhythmic chirping of crickets poured out from the tall grasses that sprawled away from the little house, and the scent of honeysuckle danced in the whispering breeze.

She breathed the sweet summer air, and for a moment, the overwhelming beauty brought a wave of serenity, which fell upon her like a great invisible blanket. Then, like someone jerking from the pull of sleep, she shook these feelings aside and made her way to her car.

Minutes later, she was driving back toward town. The sun was now deep in its descent over the rim of the horizon, and the sky seemed to catch fire as the forest took on an eerily beautiful orange hue.

Her car banged and bounced against the bad road, and she slowed a little to ease the impact on her groaning shocks. She shook her head and cursed silently as she wondered if the locals made special efforts to make the roads bad.

And then, she saw a little glint in her rearview mirror as a vehicle appeared in the road distant behind her. It was a white SUV, and it didn't seem to be in much of a hurry. But she kept her eye on it nonetheless as she drove the barren roads back to town.

Now and again, the SUV would fall out of view as she rounded a bend, only to reappear later further back behind her. She sighed a little in relief and turned her eyes on the road ahead.

A sudden flash of red blinking lights caught her attention as she neared the old railway crossing. The faint throb of an oncoming train churned like distant thunder where the tracks curved out of sight around a bend in the thick forest.

For a moment, she felt her foot grow heavy on the accelerator, her mind daring her to rush across the tracks before the engine arrived. But then, she cast the impulse aside as she felt a subtle vibration under her car wheels, a soft and yet insistent pulse that carried a promise of catastrophic mechanical might.

She stopped a safe distance from the tracks and sighed. As the chugging grew louder, she turned and looked to her left, where billowing smoke erupted into the sky over the trees.

Her gaze slid to the rearview mirror, where the approaching SUV was increasing in size. She watched as it approached and stopped behind her.

Both vehicles waited as the train edged around the bend and came into view. Tracy tapped her fingers on the steering wheel and watched as the engine chugged toward the crossing. She flinched a little as its deafening horn shrieked and thundered. Then, her head whipped back as the SUV tapped hard against her rear bumper.

In a panic, she grabbed the steering wheel with both hands and slammed hard against the brake. Tires squealed against the pavement as the SUV accelerated.

Tracy felt her heart jump into her throat as her car began to lurch forward onto the tracks. She turned to see the train bearing down on her, its horn growing into a cataclysmic roar as billowing smoke filled the air.

Terror clawed its icy fingers into her chest as she blinked at the growing locomotive, her mind paralyzed for a moment by the bone-rattling thunder of the engine.

And then, on instinct, she moved her foot from the brake and slammed it against the accelerator. The car bucked, and the wheels spun out. The train bore down, and she squinted her eyes as the tires finally bit and sent her surging across the tracks.

A shriek pierced the air as the train barreled past. Tracy skidded to a halt on the other side, her breath coming in ragged gulps, as the world seemed to spin. She shook the haze from her head, her mind caught in a dizzying vortex of fear and adrenaline.

Behind her, the train continued down the tracks, a roaring monster of steel and smoke. Through the narrow gaps between the passing train cars, she watched as the SUV turned around and drove off, its red tail lights growing smaller and smaller as it retreated in the other direction.

She sat and watched until the last train car passed, its eerie echo fading away as it rumbled off into the distance. She wiped the sweat from her forehead and took a deep, shuddering breath. Then, she put the car in drive and made a shaky drive back to town.

Chapter 9

It was just after 8 p.m. when Tracy stormed into the sheriff's office. She found him sitting at his desk reading a newspaper. And when his eyes flicked up at her, he let out an enormous, exasperated sigh.

"What now, Ms. Sterling?"

Tracy entered the room and approached his desk. She looked down at him and put her hands on her hips.

"What now, Sheriff, is someone just made an attempt on my life."

He raised his eyebrows.

"How so?"

"Less than an hour ago, I was outside of town at the railroad crossing. I stopped to wait for a passing train, and there was an SUV behind me. When the train came close, it tried to force me onto the tracks."

The sheriff looked up at her, his eyes narrowing, like a doctor giving a doubtful assessment to some sort of serial hypochondriac.

"How did it do that?"

Tracy put her hands on his desk and bent closer. She flashed her teeth as she spoke.

"It drove into me and pushed me forward onto the tracks."

The sheriff frowned.

"Did you get a license plate?"

Tracy stood up and shook her head.

"No. As soon as I realized what was happening, I drove across the tracks. The SUV was on the other side of the train, and it drove off in the other direction."

The sheriff scratched his whiskered jaw.

"You get a make? A color?"

"It was white. A Ford, I think."

The sheriff sighed again.

"A Ford, you think," he repeated.

Tracy held her hands out to her sides.

"Well?"

He shook his head.

"Well, first off, I'm glad you're alright. Second, you'll need to fill out a report."

Tracy shook her head.

"That's it?"

He shrugged.

"Fill out a report, and I'll look into it. I don't know anyone around here that drives a vehicle like that. Not off-hand, at least. But if one turns up, I'll certainly look into it. See if there's any way to corroborate your story. See if maybe there's paint on the bumper or something."

She shook her head.

"Don't bother."

He watched as she turned and went for the door.

"You mind if I ask what you were doing out that way in the first place?" he said as she reached for the doorknob.

"Yes," she said as she walked out the door.

She stepped outside and let the door shut behind her. The very last of the light was leaking from the sky, and streetlights were popping on as the foot traffic thinned.

She took a deep breath while the rage and frustration seeped from her body. Then, her brows pinched together as she saw Carter walking down the other side of the street. The young man seemed to be moving with purpose, his footsteps hurried as he passed all the little shops and restaurants.

Tracy stepped back and watched as the young man turned down a little alleyway between a barbershop and a hardware store. When he vanished from sight, she looked all around and crossed the street, her pace picking up as she half-jogged after him.

As she approached the edge of the alley, she stopped and peaked around the corner. Down the dusty, narrow path, there stood a shaggy-looking young man about the same age as Carter. He was very thin and pale, and he smoked a cigarette as he watched Carter approach. The two gave each other a nod, and Tracy strained to listen as they traded words.

"What time are we all meeting?" Carter asked.

The other young man thought for a moment.

"I guess I'm heading up to the old Douglas place at around midnight," he replied in a raspy voice. "You can ride with me."

Carter nodded and gestured for the young man's cigarette. He passed it over, and they smoked together in silence. Then, they gave each other another silent nod, and Carter started back up the alley.

Cursing silently, Tracy retreated backward and turned away. As Carter's footsteps crunched on the dirt floor of the little alley, she hurried over to the barbershop and opened the door. A little brass bell chimed as she stepped inside, where the old barber was shaving a patron with a straight-edged razor.

The barber's head jerked up, and the patron flinched.

"Shit!" he cried as he clutched at his throat.

The barber looked down where the razor had nicked the man's neck.

"Oh, goodness," he said. "I'm so sorry, Henry."

They both looked up at Tracy, who swallowed and frowned.

"I'm sorry. I didn't mean to startle you."

The barber turned his attention back to his customer and started dabbing at the cut with a towel. Tracy turned and looked out the glass door, but Carter had already walked a good distance in the other direction down the street. She sighed and turned back around.

"Could I possibly ask you gentlemen a question?"

The two men looked at her.

"I'm about to close," said the barber. "You need a haircut?"

Tracy looked at the man in the chair, who grimaced as he clutched the towel against his neck, the white fibers turning pink near the wound.

"No," said Tracy. "Thanks anyway. I just have a question."

The barber furrowed his brows.

"Alright."

Tracy smiled politely.

"Can you tell me how I might get to the old Douglas place?"

The barber exchanged a look with the man in the chair.

"What in the hell for?" he asked. "It's just a bunch of rubble."

Tracy assumed a look of naïve innocence.

"Well, I'm a bit of an amateur photographer. And I'm interested in taking some photographs of the old buildings around here. They're quite compelling."

He frowned thoughtfully.

"Well, I don't see no beauty in the place. But if you want to see for yourself, head up Doogan Rd, about ten miles. Then, take a left on Pilot Rd. Then, take another left on Cornwallis and take that another twenty miles or so. The old Douglas place is on the right side, down a short stretch of road. You'll have to watch for it, though. Cause it's damn near been swallowed up by the woods."

Tracy smiled and nodded.

"Oh, thank you so much."

The barber looked her over one last time.

"You sure you don't want a cut?"

Tracy shook her head.

"If I change my mind, you'll be the first to know."

He grunted and turned back toward the man in the chair, while Tracy walked out the door and hurried back to her hotel room.

She spent the next few hours pacing the floor of her room, her mind at work as she re-lived every interaction with Carter. She thought about his words, the way he spoke them. The way his eyes never seemed to focus, his clothes, his bad breath, the way he wore his hair. And all the while, she watched the clock, which seemed endowed with the supernatural might to resist the pull of time.

At last, just before midnight, she got into her car and started up Doogan Rd, which ran away from the town into the deep low country, not far from where Caroline Duncan had been found.

As she moved away from civilization, a growing disquiet began to fester within her mind, every curve and twist tightening the knots of apprehension as she navigated the labyrinthine country lanes. Something wasn't right about Carter. She felt it in her bones. And as she passed through the tree-lined corridors, a quiet little voice nagged her to turn around.

This, she quieted with a big breath and a deep frown, her eyes narrowing as she peered through the windshield, where her headlights bathed the bad roads as insects darted all about.

After several minutes, she made all the necessary turns and spotted a sudden turnoff that veered off the beaten road and into a narrow track shrouded by forest.

Tracy slowed and paused for a moment, her mind considering all the choices that had led her to this point and the ones that lay ahead. She took another breath and made the turn.

Her car bucked a little as it moved onto the narrow dirt path, a shriek piercing the night as a low-hanging branch raked her hood. As she pressed forward, old trees reached out overhead, their gnarled branches weaving a canopy of shadows that devoured the moonlight.

The old, pockmarked road ran deep into the forested swampland, and her tires throbbed and shook as they struggled with the rough terrain. Deeper she drove into the dark woods, where the world seemed to hold its breath, surrendering to an eerie stillness that sent cold shivers up Tracy's spine.

At last, she saw a break in the overgrowth and extinguished her headlights. Rolling forward at a creep, she saw an old, dilapidated house lift from the darkness. All around it, several other cars parked in a makeshift clearing, their chrome bodies glistening under the ghostly kiss of moonlight.

She stopped her car and killed the engine. She watched and waited for several minutes. Then, she opened the door and quietly stepped out into the night.

Up the narrow road she walked, her weight on her toes as if she moved upon dancer's feet. Somewhere along the way, her hand unconsciously felt for her pistol. And when it came away empty, she snatched up a branch from the ground. This she held tightly in her right hand as she reached the end of the path.

She paused in the shadows and looked over the old house. The skeletal structure was draped in a patchwork of peeling paint and rotten wood, its broken windows like dark, empty eyes. In front of it, there were four cars parked in a gravelly swath a few yards from the crumbling entrance.

She held her ground and scanned the area, but no one seemed to be stirring outside. And then, she saw a flicker of firelight within one of the ruined windows. Without thinking, she crept from the obscurity of the shadows and out into the moonlight. With every step, the crunch of gravel felt thunderous, invasive, and she held her breath as she approached the exterior of the dilapidated house.

When she reached the structure, she stood and breathed the humid air, eyes darting about, knuckles white as she squeezed the length of wood. Seconds passed, but she heard no voices. No footsteps. Nothing but the crickets, which chirped in their millions amid the endless smothering black.

Another flicker of firelight in the window.

Tracy turned and crept closer, her fingers grazing the wood exterior as she approached the broken window pane. She held her breath as she scanned the scene unfolding within.

The sickly, flickering glow of an oil lamp barely illuminated the room, casting long, monstrous shadows that danced and writhed against the moldy walls. Amid that weak orange light, upon a bare concrete floor, six young men sat in a clump, their gaunt faces and hollow eyes appearing ghostly in the limited light.

She saw Carter among them, a makeshift pipe in his hand. The sharp, noxious smell of methamphetamine wafted through the broken window, and she struggled to withstrain a cough. A deep sadness spread within her chest as she watched them trade the pipe. This was a den of addiction, a pit of despair, and she was standing on the precipice, staring into the abyss.

A little cough escaped the fence of her teeth, and her heart froze as the men whipped their heads toward the sound. Their glazed eyes, wide with paranoia, bore into the window, but she had already retreated back into the dark night.

Without pausing, she spun on her heel and sprinted back towards her car. Her footfalls crunched audibly against the gravel, the underbrush clawing at her jeans as she fled.

Reaching her car, she wrenched open the door and threw herself inside, her fingers fumbling to jam the key into the ignition. The faint sound of voices filled the air, as the men spilled out of the crumbling structure. Tracy's key found its mark, and the car roared to life. She slammed the shifter into reverse, and gravel crunched under the spin of tires as she backed down the way she'd come. The grim spectacle faded away behind a haze of dust in her fading headlights. And then, she was back out on the road and turning toward town.

She hit the gas, and the car rushed forward, the tires thumping against unseen divots as she sped down the old barren road. She didn't look back. But dark thoughts clawed at the edges of her mind. Carter surrounded by the hollow-eyed men in that decaying house, the hopeless quiet as they all stared vacantly at the walls and the floor.

She tried to shake away the thought, her eyes straining to focus as she navigated the winding forest road back toward town. The miles disappeared behind her, while her car split a path through the silhouettes of towering bald cypress and live oak trees, which shut away the moonlight with a canopy of fluttering leaves.

With every mile, the forest seemed to gobble her up like a great beast devouring its tiny prey. Deeper and deeper, she pushed into the swallowing black, her headlights carving twin tunnels into the darkness while her tires stirred up ghostly plumes of dust that danced in the wake of her car's rumble.

She flinched and cursed as her vehicle jerked violently, the shocks groaning under the strain of a deep rut chiseled by years of harsh weather. The car skidded a little and then straightened, as the tires found traction. She shook her head and frowned as little clouds of insects fogged the headlights, some exploding against her windshield like some gruesome form of abstract art. Her lip wrinkled up as she smeared them away with her wipers.

Then, she straightened as a glint of light sparkled in the rearview mirror.

The glint quickly morphed into a pair of bright headlights, their beams cutting through the darkness like two fiery eyes. She swallowed and watched as the lights grew larger. Then, there came an ominous rumble, like the growl of some predatory beast, as Beaux Parker's red pickup truck closed in behind her.

Instinctively, Tracy's fingers moved toward her gun. She sighed when they came away empty and then seized her phone. As she tapped buttons, the truck driver ignited the vehicle's high beams, and Tracy squinted as she struggled to dial while keeping her car on the road.

She cursed at the call failure message as the no service indicator appeared in the corner of the screen. She tossed the phone aside and adjusted her mirror, so the glare of Beaux's headlights moved off her face. Narrowing her eyes at the coming road, she jammed her foot against the gas pedal. A gap began to grow between the two vehicles, Tracy's car shaking violently as the tires bounced against the potholes and loose clods of hard earth.

As the trees whirred by, she glanced at her side mirror, where the truck was growing in size as it consumed the space between them. She flinched as the vehicle roared within inches of her rear bumper, its horn blaring through the desolate darkness, headlights flickering from low to high.

Tracy's grip tightened on the steering wheel, her pulse quickening in anticipation of a collision. But instead, the truck fell back at the last moment, the horn continuing to pollute the quiet with blast after sickening blast.

Again, the lights blinded her eyes as the truck raced forward. She jolted in her seat as the grill of the pickup tapped her rear bumper. The car yawed a little, and Tracy struggled to keep it on the narrow road, her knuckles whitening as she pressed her foot down on the accelerator.

The dirt and gravel pinged against the underside of her car as space grew between the vehicles. And then, in what seemed like an instant, the truck was right on her tail again.

A wide stretch of road opened up ahead, and the pickup's engine made a throaty growl as it veered off the road and into the shoulder, where it maneuvered next to Tracy and veered toward her. Gritting her teeth, she slammed on the brakes, narrowly avoiding a collision as the pickup moved into the road ahead of her. And then, brake lights flared red, as the pickup slammed to a stop.

In a panic, Tracy jammed her shoe down and brought her car to a stop, the front bumper glancing against the truck as her body flung forward hard against the seatbelt.

Almost immediately, every door in the truck opened. Tracy looked up to see men rushing to both sides of her vehicle. She put her hand on the gear shifter and started to put the car in reverse. But her hand froze when she saw Beaux Parker holding a gun outside her window.

"Out of the car," he said. "Right now."

Instinctively, Tracy moved toward her pistol, and her heart sank as it came away empty again. She brought her hand away from the shifter and opened the door.

"What is this?" she asked as she stepped out into the hot, humid night.

Beaux aimed the gun at her, and his face lit up with a wicked grin.

"It's payback time," he said. "That's what."

On the other side of the car, his two friends chuckled. Tracy glanced at them and then turned back to Beaux, who was now looking her up and down with a thoughtful face.

"Hmm," he said. "You've got a nice little body on you. I didn't notice that before."

She felt his eyes travel over her body, and something inside told her to run. Instead, she grinned up at him.

"You're not so bad yourself."

He looked up at her and furrowed his brow, his head tilting like a flummoxed dog. And then, with a calm and sudden movement, she reached for the gun and took it by the barrel.

Beaux shrieked in pain as she leveraged the gun inward, bending his wrist in an awkward position. She twisted upward, while his screams filled the night. But somehow, he maintained a grip on the weapon, even as she twisted and pulled.

Now, bootsteps crunched the gravel behind her, as the other two men hurried around the car. In a panic, she released the gun and scrambled off the road, her body vanishing into the woods while Beaux screamed at his friends.

"Get that bitch!"

Their voices trailed away as Tracy plunged into the boggy wilderness, adrenaline fueling her legs as she moved through the enveloping shroud of woods.

Whip-like branches lashed her arms and legs as she blindly pushed into the tangled forest, her shoes plunging into the muddy bottoms, which sucked greedily at her soles.

All around her, bullfrogs croaked in the darkness, their deep groans joined by unseen insects that seeded the winds with a chorus of alien chirps.

Behind her, the distant sound of men's voices haunted the darkness, while flashlights cast ghostly specters that danced within the gloom.

A flickering beam momentarily illuminated the path ahead, and Tracy froze, her heart thundering within her chest. She waited in the darkness until it veered away. And then, she ran on, her footfalls sloppy and smacking as they rang against the wet earth.

Deeper and deeper, she ran into the humid labyrinth of the insect-ridden night, the path dissolving into a maze of dense vegetation.

With arms outstretched, she navigated through the swamp's thorny embrace, each whip of a branch across her skin a stinging red rebuke.

The swamp exhaled its wet breath against her, heavy with the pungency of rotting matter. Her heart thumped erratically in her chest, her lungs gasping for air in the stench-laden humidity, the taste on her tongue a cocktail of decaying leaves and sour waters.

After several minutes of difficult progress, she slowed her pace momentarily, gulping down the foul air as she tried to quell the fire in her chest.

Laughter again. Only closer this time.

A snap echoed from nearby, and Tracy forced herself onward, her shoes sinking into the muck as she fought her way through the dense green wall. Snatching vines tugged at her clothing while more branches lashed at her face, scratching red trails onto her perspiring skin.

Her legs propelled her forward almost mechanically, despite the weight of exhaustion that began to drain her strength. And then her foot caught a gnarled tree root, and she felt herself falling. Face first, she sprawled onto the slimy earth, a small gasp slipping from between her lips despite her best efforts.

"Over there!" echoed a voice.

Drained and desperate, Tracy fumbled in the silt and undergrowth, searching for a branch or a stone to use for defense. Instead, she found only squirming insects, their wet, swollen bodies wiggling in her fingers as they nestled against her trembling skin. As if poked by something electric, she jerked her hand away and struggled to rise, her muscles screaming in protest as she began running again at a slow, fatigued pace.

Footfalls echoed in her ears, their ominous resonance shattering the silence as they grew louder and louder behind her. And then, a firm hand materialized from the darkness, closing around her arm. Without a sound, she tore herself free and retaliated instinctively. Her sharp elbow connected with something solid, extracting a grunt of pain from the darkness. And then, she was free.

A surge of adrenaline lent her new strength, and she tore through the marshy undergrowth, each squelching footfall mimicking the frantic rhythm of her heart. The pursuers followed, their profanity-laden grunts audible amid the orchestra of nocturnal life.

The woods grew denser now, and the gnarled roots of ancient cypress trees seemed to lunge from all directions, like skeletal hands snatching at her feet from the murky depths.

The voices of her pursuers grew fainter, and she allowed herself to slow somewhat. And then, her foot hit a root cloaked beneath the thick carpet of rotting leaves, and she catapulted into a clearing. She raised her face from the forest floor and spat foul soil from her mouth. She looked at the little clearing, a soggy carpet of tall swamp grass beneath the glow of moonlight.

Tracy winced as she tried to regain her breath, the sharp taste of sweat and brackish water intermingling on her lips. She tried to get to her feet, but before she could even raise to a knee, the silence was shattered by the sound of cracking twigs.

Shadows shifted at the edge of the clearing. And then, the beam of a flashlight slashed through the darkness, its harsh light sweeping over the clearing and fixing on Tracy. Cold fear surged through her veins as the flashlight's owner stepped into the clearing.

"Gotcha," said Beaux Parker, his deep voice laced with a chilling satisfaction.

Frantic, Tracy rose to her feet, her heart pounding in her chest as she looked all around. From the edges of her eyes, she saw two more flashlights, their beams cutting through the darkness, closing in on her. The night swallowed her hopes as she found herself encircled.

"Now, we get to have a little fun," said Beaux as he took a step forward.

Tracy backed away, her fists clenched at her sides. And then she felt two big arms encircle her from behind. Gasping, she drove her elbow into the assailant's ribs, and he squawked as he fell away.

"Fuck!" he yelled as he clutched at his side.

Like a cornered animal, Tracy spun in circles, her teeth flashing white as she regarded each of the three men with wild, feral eyes.

"There's nowhere to go, " said Beaux.

His face was illuminated in the ghastly glow of the flashlight, his grin wolfish.

Silently, Tracy assessed the men, her mind whirring for a plan, any plan. As one of them stepped closer, she spun to face him. And then spun again as another advanced from behind.

"Calm down, now," said Beaux as he put his hands up. "You're just making this harder on yourself."

He took a heavy step toward her, and when she turned, the other two men seized her arms.

"There we go," said Beaux as his face lit up with a wide grin.

Tracy tried to jerk free, but the men held her arms with vice-like strength.

"Whoa, whoa," said Beaux. "Calm down."

"Let me go," she hissed.

He raised his eyebrows.

"Not until we have some fun." He approached and ran a calloused hand across her cheek. "I know we haven't been friends up to this point. But it's not too late. I like a strong woman like you. They got legs like vice grips."

His two friends chuckled for a moment. And then their voices fell silent as Tracy lunged forward and spat into Beaux's face.

The big man stepped back and wiped the saliva from his cheeks. Without a word, he stepped forward and drove his fist into her stomach. With a low, mournful cry, Tracy folded over, and the two men let her fall to the ground.

They laughed as her mouth opened and closed like a fish on land, her lungs sucking fruitlessly, as if all the world's air had been lost into the vacuum of space.

"Now," said Beaux. "It's time to teach you a little lesson."

He took a step closer and kicked her in the face. A loud crunch detonated in the woods as she felt her nose give way. The world went silent as Tracy's head exploded with bright flashes of light. She tried to roll away, but her breath had not yet returned, so she flopped around and wept silently as blood boiled out from her broken face.

The men laughed as they took turns kicking her. And then they stepped back and watched as she coughed and gasped.

"God damn," said one of the men as Tracy began to crawl.

They stood and watched as she pulled herself away, an inch at a time, like some robotic thing, driven only by programming to survive at all costs.

Beaux shook his head and approached. With gritted teeth, he stomped on her back and grinned as she fell flat on her face. He hooked the toe of his boot beneath her stomach, and a low moan tumbled from her lips as he flipped her over onto her back.

"You don't quit. I'll give you that."

One of the other men approached and dropped to his knees. His belt was already unbuckled, and he licked his lips as he began to tug down Tracy's pants.

"No," said Beaux. "We're only supposed to send a message."

The man cursed and stood, his belt buckle ringing as he refastened his pants.

Tracy blinked up at the stars as they all stood over her, their hulking silhouettes like demons to her woozy, fragmented mind.

"Let's see how you do spending the night in the swamp," said Beaux. "Then, we'll see if you're ready to go on back home."

One of the other men looked at him.

"What if a gator gets her?"

Beaux shrugged.

"All the better."

With that, they turned and walked away, their echoing laughter growing fainter and fainter until it vanished entirely, leaving only the sounds of insect calls and stirring wildlife.

And Tracy heard the wild things rustling in the darkness as she sucked the sour air with shallow stabbing breaths. Until, at last, she fell into the embrace of merciful sleep, where she endured the swamp and all its terrors enclosed amid the heavy arms of oblivion, as tiny creatures probed her body, and clouds of mosquitoes devoured the red nectar weeping from her open wounds.

Chapter 10

Tracy breathed in and opened one eye. Everything was blurry, and she blinked and blinked as consciousness returned like a hard wave crashing against the shore. At last, the haze fell away, and she could see white ceiling tiles overhead. Bright light stabbed down at her one open eye, as nausea swam within her stomach. She nearly gagged at the scent of disinfectant, which mingled with the unmistakable sounds of hospital life. A heart monitor beeped and hummed. Nurses shuffled down linoleum-covered corridors, their shoes squeaking on the polished floors.

Someone was talking to her, but her mind could not interpret the words. She turned her head, and pain exploded within her body. A little cry escaped her cracked lips, and a hand fell upon her arm.

"Hey, hey," said the voice. "Take it easy."

She turned her head and blinked at her surroundings, the world crystallizing through only one eye, the other black and bruised and sealed by swollen flesh. She coughed and cringed as excruciating pain knifed through her chest.

Howard looked at her and swallowed, her battered form reflected in the lawyer's wide somber eyes.

"Relax," he said. "You're severely injured."

Tracy took in air with tiny little sips, a tear trickling out her bad eye.

"What happened?" she whispered.

Howard swallowed hard as he frowned down at her.

"Someone found your car on the side of the road. The sheriff organized a search party, I guess. Him and a couple of the locals. They found you in the woods just after dawn. You were in bad shape, Tracy. They gave you some painkillers and a sedative and brought you to the hospital. I came as soon as I heard. You've been asleep all day."

He paused and took in a slow breath.

"The doctor says you've got some broken ribs, and your kidneys are bruised. Your nose is broken, and you may have a concussion."

He shook his head.

"What are you still doing here, Tracy?"

She swallowed.

"Looking for Caroline's killer."

Her voice came out like a whisper, and Howard had to lean in close to hear. He shook his head and swallowed.

"It's over, Tracy. There's nothing you can do here. I should have never sent you out here. You just need to leave things to me now."

She breathed and grimaced, a little moan escaping her lips as her chest moved.

"What about Beaux Parker?" she asked.

Howard sat back in his chair.

"The sheriff says he'll look into it. But Beaux and his friends are nowhere to be seen. He said I ought to take you home and let him handle things."

Tracy almost laughed as another tear slipped from her eye.

"Bullshit," she whispered. "He's owned by Bill Parker. This entire town is. As soon as we leave, the whole thing will get swept under the rug."

Howard leaned forward and clasped his hands together.

"Tracy, I know you want justice, for yourself, for that girl. But that justice needs to come in a court. You need to put your faith in the law."

She looked at him, and he flinched a little at what he saw in her one open eye.

"What are you going to do?" she asked. "You don't have any evidence to clear Caroline's boyfriend. He's going to rot in prison."

Howard shook his head.

"You've never seen me in court," he said as he forced a weak smile.

Tracy shook her head, and Howard's face grew somber.

"Listen, Tracy. You need to let this go. You've done what you can. Sometimes, things just don't work out, no matter what you try. Sometimes, the bad guys win. And there's just nothing you can do about it."

She shook her head.

"I don't accept that."

He swallowed and looked at her.

"Let me tell you a story, if you'll allow it."

She sighed and shook her head.

"Please," he said. "Just listen."

She looked up at him, and he took a deep breath.

"Back when I was knee-deep in law textbooks," he said, "I had this burning urge to become a prosecutor. The kind that locks up the villains and makes the world a cleaner place. One day, I'm shooting the breeze with the judge I was interning for, and I tell him about my dream. He gives me this look and says, "Kid, why don't you spend a morning in criminal court? Get a taste of the real deal." I figure, why not?

"So, there I am in this jam-packed courtroom, with back-to-back hearings lined up. And let me tell you, it's a circus. The attorneys on both sides look like they've just rolled out of bed. They're mixing up witness names, clearly swamped and, to be honest, looking like they'd rather be anywhere else.

"I remember this one kid, couldn't be older than twenty, getting charged with selling drugs to kids and some outstanding warrant and carrying a gun without a permit. Before the hearing, his lawyer and the prosecutor are off to the side, yukking it up like old college buddies. Next thing I know, they've cut a deal, and the kid's practically walking away with nothing more than a warning."

He looked off into space for a moment. Then, he sighed and looked back at her.

"So, later, the judge asks me my thoughts. And I admitted I felt a little disillusioned. I waited for him to tell me something to make me feel better. Instead, you know what he said? He told me to imagine two sides of the city. He said, on one side, you've got the wealthy, the powerful. They live in their glass towers, untouched, unscathed by the chaos that brews on the streets below. Then, on the other side, there

98

are the other folks, the ones trying to scrape by, living paycheck to paycheck, hustling just to stay afloat.

"In this city, the judge says, there's a bridge that connects the two worlds. Now, the judge tells me to imagine that a man from the poorer side steals a loaf of bread to feed his family. He's caught and sentenced harshly. Next, a rich man is caught embezzling millions. He hires a slick lawyer, gets a slap on the wrist."

Tracy frowned up at him.

"A judge told you this?"

Howard nodded.

"He told me more than that. He told me there is no justice. Not really, at least. He said, we can arrest and jail the thieves, the murderers, the drug dealers. But we can't arrest poverty. And we can't handcuff corruption or lock up the societal flaws that drive people to commit crime in the first place.

"He said we aren't heroes in some tale. We're janitors, cleaning up the mess without ever fixing the broken machine that keeps spewing it out. He said his job is to keep the peace, keep the city from tearing itself apart. That and nothing more."

He leaned back and shook her head at her.

"Justice is a beautiful dream, Tracy. But trust me. I've been in the justice business a long time. And it's just that—a dream. The true power isn't in our hands. It's in the hands of those who write the rules, who decide which side of the bridge gets the short end of the stick. We do what we can. And when we reach the end of our ability. We have to bow out. It's the way it is. The world is a sick place. You try to do as much good as you can. But it's a losing battle. Especially if you don't know when to quit on a lost cause."

Tracy looked at him and shook her head.

"I don't believe you really feel that way. Not in your heart."

He looked down at the floor and shook his head.

"I believe in what's real, Tracy. Anything else is a waste of time. Trying to save the world is like using a teaspoon to empty the ocean. It's just not possible."

She shook her head.

"I'm not leaving, Howard. Not until I see this through."

He looked up at her and held his hands out to his side.

"Tracy, you were almost killed. And now you can barely breathe. How are you going to even function? And even if you could function, the sheriff says he still has an open case against you. And there are people here that seem willing to kill you."

She moved a little and grimaced, her battered face wrinkling up as she breathed through her teeth.

"I don't care," she said. "You and that judge can believe what you need to believe, so you can put your weapons down and go on with your lives. But I'm not wired that way. Not yet, at least. This shit isn't over. Not until I'm satisfied. And I'm a long fucking way from satisfaction."

Howard sat back and looked at her, his head shaking slowly. It was quiet, except for the high-pitched squeak leaking out from Tracy's bandaged nose.

"Alright," he said as he removed his cell phone.

Tracy looked at him.

"What are you doing?"

He frowned at her.

"If you're serious about this, I need to make a call."

Chapter 11

It was coming up on midnight, and the forest was dark beneath the moonless summer night. In the dense recesses of the backwoods near the edge of the quarry, an old cabin sat alone amid a tangle of gnarled bushes and twisted trees. Outside, weeds had begun to claim its exterior, their winding tendrils curling high upon the walls, as if some great tentacled beast searched blindly for a grip with which to pull the structure down into the swampy depths.

That was on the outside.

Inside, it was a nice little place, considerately appointed with three big cots, which were sheeted with white linens that were crisp and clean and neatly made.

Or, they had been before Beaux and his friends moved in. Now, they were yellow in spots. And the whole place stank of male sweat and other foul secretions. Empty beer cans littered the floor, and dirty clothes were piled high in one corner. Plump horse flies circled in the hot, humid air, and the men took turns swatting them away as they sat around a small wooden table.

Beaux watched each of his friends with a wide grin, a deck of dog-eared playing cards in his hands as he regarded each with disgust.

"You two aren't fit to sit at the same table as me," he said.

The men glanced at each other and shook their heads.

"Just deal, will you?"

The flickering light from a single oil lamp danced in his dark eyes, and his grin widened as he began tossing cards.

"As you wish."

The men collected their cards and looked them over. Beaux watched as they frowned at their hands.

"How many you need?" he asked.

"Three," said one of the men.

"Two," said the other.

He gave them their cards.

"And I'll take two myself," he said.

They watched as he dealt himself a pair of fresh cards.

"How long are we gonna have to stay in this place?" asked one of the men.

Beaux scowled as he looked at his cards.

"You'd better settle in. It's only been three damn days. Daddy says we have to lay low a while. Then, if the bitch still ain't got the message, we hit her again. This time harder."

The other young man looked at his own cards and shook his head.

"If that happens, I'm gonna get me a piece. You ain't stopping me again."

Beaux raised his eyebrows as he looked down at his pile of cash.

"Maybe we'll all get a piece," he said.

He tossed a hundred-dollar bill onto the pile of cash in the middle of the table. The two other men looked at each other.

"I'm out," said one as he tossed his cards face down.

The other man shook his head.

"That ain't fair, Beaux. You know we ain't got the money for them kind of stakes."

Beaux shrugged.

"Ain't my problem. You in or out?"

The young man looked at his cards and chewed his teeth. He swallowed hard and looked at the dwindling stack of cash beneath his chin. He sighed and tossed his cards away.

"I'm out."

Beaux grinned as he raked the money to his side of the table. His two friends shook their heads as they tipped back their beers.

"How do you know the sheriff ain't gonna come out here lookin for us?" one asked. "This cabin ain't exactly hidden. It's right next to the quarry, for Christ's sake. Anyone with a little sense would think to come check here."

Beaux shook his head as he counted his money.

"Ain't no one comin out here," he said. "They know better than to fuck with Daddy. Anyways, the sheriff knows his place. He ain't gonna stick his nose into my family's business. Hell, I could walk right through town, and there ain't shit he could do about it. Daddy's just having us stay out here to keep up appearances until that bitch PI leaves town. There ain't nothin to worry about."

He grinned as he reached for his beer.

"Anyways, I hope she don't leave."

The other two nodded.

"She's got a nice ass on her. I'll give her that," said one of the men. "Although I doubt her face will still look good after what we done to it."

Beaux chuckled a little as he sucked from his can. He set the beer down and ran the back of his hand over his mouth.

"Just push her face down in the mud," he said. "As long as her ass is up, that's all I need."

The other men laughed and then fell silent as a fist knocked against the door.

"Who the fuck is that?" one whispered.

Beaux shrugged.

"Relax," he said. "It's probably daddy's boys with some fresh supplies."

He stood up as the fist slammed against the door again. The other men traded glances, while Beaux crossed the room and reached for the knob.

He opened the door and frowned.

A large man stood outside, his eyes looking out from under a pair of low lids. Beaux looked the man over, and his brows lowered as he gave the stranger a thoughtful assessment.

The man had a big bald head and a jaw covered with coarse gray whiskers. His cheeks were slightly pock-marked, and his nose was more than a little off-center. He was in his late forties at least, maybe early fifties. But none of that stole from his imposing size.

"Who the fuck are you?" asked Beaux.

The man said nothing, his face without expression, as if he were perpetually bored of this and all things. A quiet man with a quiet pulse. And a mind unencumbered by the rules of men or the restrictive burdens of moral thought.

Chapter 12

Howard paced around the little cabin, his face pointed down at his phone while he tapped his thumbs against the screen. He paused and looked across the room, where Tracy sat on the little sofa. Her breathing had gotten better since they left the hospital. Deeper and more productive, each inhalation no longer caused her to flinch, though the rest of her looked worse than ever.

Somehow her battered face had grown even larger on one side, and the bruises on her cheeks had taken on a yellowish tinge at the edges, where her one bad eye remained hidden within a hideous mass of swollen flesh.

He frowned and set his phone down on the nightstand.

"Can I get you anything?" he asked. "Some water."

She glared at him with her only working eye.

"I'm fine."

He nodded and sat down on one of the twin beds. He looked around the room. On one far wall, there was a painting of a man in waders fly fishing for trout in a mountain stream. On the other, a taxidermied deer head laughed down with a set of dark black demonic eyes. Howard loosened his tie and pulled it away from his collar.

"Well," he said. "We should be good here a couple more days. I told the sheriff I'd take you home as soon as you were feeling a little better."

Tracy shifted in her seat and winced as she clutched her ribs.

"Lovely," she said.

Howard leaned forward and propped his forearms against his knees.

"What is your plan here, Tracy?"

She looked at him, and he seemed to almost recoil at the sight of her.

"There's a man I need to talk to."

He furrowed his brows.

"Who?"

"A potential witness."

She started to stand, and Howard's face advertised concern.

"You're not leaving now?"

She steadied herself and limped over to the dresser, where a bottle of pills sat next to a glass of water and Howard's car keys.

"You just said we only have a few days," she said as she cracked open the bottle. "We've already wasted two sitting in this fucking cabin. I need to get going."

He watched as she opened the bottle and swallowed two of the pills. He checked his watch and frowned.

"Don't go just yet," he said.

She swallowed a gulp of water and looked at him.

"Why?"

His eyes moved to the door and then back to hers.

"Just wait a little while longer," he said. "A few minutes."

She narrowed her eyes and turned to face him.

"What's going on, Howard?"

He started to speak, but a fist knocked against the door. They both looked at each other, and then Tracy backed up toward the nightstand.

"Hold on," said Howard.

He held a hand up as if trying to calm a panicked animal. She watched as he moved toward the door. She opened her mouth to speak, but he silenced her with a finger.

"Just wait," he said.

He approached the door and began opening it without looking through the peephole. She opened her mouth to protest and then stopped as Jimmy walked in.

He looked around, his eyes falling on her battered face. He sighed and shook his head.

"You look like shit, kid."

Tracy stared at him with her one functioning eye.

"Jimmy, what are you doing here?"

He shrugged.

"Howard said you could use a hand."

She looked at Howard, who gave an apologetic half-smile.

"Sorry," said the lawyer. "I thought it would be for the best."

Tracy looked at Jimmy.

"I thought you wouldn't fly."

He shook his head.

"I didn't. I drove. Twelve fucking hours. You owe me, kid."

She looked down and shook her head.

"I didn't want to get you wrapped up in this."

He raised his eyebrows.

"You let me worry about me."

She forced a crooked smile as he approached and looked her over.

"You look like shit," he said.

She raised her chin and looked at him, one eye almost completely swollen shut.

"I gave as good as I got."

Jimmy nodded.

"I believe it."

"Anyway," she said. "I'm not finished with them yet."

Jimmy shrugged.

"You'll have to wait a while. They'll be in the hospital for a few days at least."

Tracy raised her eyebrows.

"What did you do?"

He scratched his whiskered jaw.

"I just finished what you started."

Tracy looked at Howard, who put his hands up.

"I didn't see anything. I didn't hear anything."

Tracy shook her head and turned toward Jimmy.

"Jimmy, you shouldn't have gotten involved like that. What if they ID you?"

He looked at her with his expressionless face.

"They'd have to wake up to do that. Anyway, I don't plan to be here long enough for it to matter."

She swallowed and sniffed a little.

"Thanks, Jimmy."

He nodded and looked her over. He approached and put a hand to her cheek, his jaw clenching as he assessed her bruised and battered face.

"What the hell are you doing out here, Tracy?"

She looked up at him.

"Trying to solve a murder."

He let go of her face and stepped back.

"There's plenty of murders at home. You don't have to go prospecting."

"It's my fault," said Howard. "I didn't know what I was getting her into."

Tracy shook her head.

"It's nobody's fault. I should have been more careful. This place is probably one of the most corrupt places you'll ever find. There's no law. No real law. The sheriff is just an extension of this Bill Parker, who runs everything. It's all just puppets."

Jimmy frowned as Tracy gave him the whole story, or at least the parts that Howard hadn't already explained. As for the lawyer, he just sat listening with a dumbfounded look on his face, his head shaking from time to time as she went over the past few days.

"Jesus," he said when she'd finished.

Jimmy looked at him and then looked back at Tracy.

"Well," he said. "It sounds like you've done all you can, and there aren't many more cards to play. So, why don't you go home and leave this place to rot?"

Tracy looked up at him as if he'd suggested she jump in front of a subway train.

"I can't just leave," she said.

"I don't know, Tracy," said Howard. "I think Jimmy may be right. There are too many obstacles here. The sheriff has a real case against you. And he has the authority to put you behind bars."

She turned toward him.

"What about your client?" she asked.

Howard sighed.

"I'll do the best I can with what I've got. That's what lawyering is. There's not a ton of evidence. I might be able to plea bargain with the DA. Get a reasonable deal for a confession. He may have to spend a few years in prison. But it won't be the rest of his life."

She looked at them both and shook her head.

"I'm not going to let this poor boyfriend spend a decade in a South Carolina prison for a crime he didn't commit."

Jimmy held a hand out to his side.

"How do you know he didn't do it?"

"Because," she said. "Beaux Parker did it. He and his friends killed Caroline. I know it."

"How do you know?" asked Jimmy. "You don't have any real evidence tying him to the crime. You only know that he's a violent asshole. Maybe it really was the boyfriend. Maybe they do have the right guy. Or maybe it was this brother you told me about. Maybe he resented her for getting out of this place. Hell, I know I would, and I've only been here a day."

"No," said Tracy. "It's Beaux Parker. I know it."

Jimmy shook his head.

"You don't know it. What you know is that you hate that boy. And you have the right. For what he did to you. For who he is. You should hate him. I hate him too. But you don't know if he killed that girl. You don't have any evidence at all. Your brain is clouded with hate."

Howard nodded.

"He's right, Tracy. Listen, I want to believe that all my clients are innocent. But that's not always the case. Now, I will do my best to get him the best possible deal. But there is no real evidence tying anyone else to this crime. Not yet, at least."

Tracy pointed up to her face.

"Look at me, Howard. Does this look like something an innocent person would do? If they had nothing to do with this murder, why are they trying to get rid of me? Answer me that. Why would they be so worried about a PI digging around in their business?"

Howard bent over and propped his forearms on his knees.

"Look, if what Bill Parker told you about potential rare earth minerals is true, there are definitely large corporations that would be highly interested in his quarry. Particularly those involved in technology, automotive, defense or renewable energy. This is especially true given the geopolitical considerations surrounding these minerals, most of which are mined in China right now.

"Now, from what I understand, it's pretty common for large corporations to buy the rights to a mineral deposit rather than set up their own mining operations, especially if the corporation doesn't have mining experience. Or if they want to fast-track the process, or if the quarry owner doesn't want to sell his entire operation. So, that means any deal probably means Parker stays on to do the mining. But there would be a whole lot of hoops to jump through first."

He looked at each of them in turn.

"I'm not an expert, but I do know that before a corporation decides to buy the rights to his quarry, they would likely want to conduct extensive testing to verify the existence and quantity of the minerals. But it wouldn't end there. They'd also want to make sure Parker was on the up and up, at least to their standards, which admittedly may not be very high. But even still, mining rare earth minerals is very messy. It means the local area gets a lot of toxic shit in their waterways. And it could mean this whole town gets bought up and torn down. That means they'd have to get approval from various regulatory bodies without attracting unwanted attention from community members and environmental groups. Any kind of nefarious activity could blow the deal, whether it's illegal chemical dumps in a local river or outright criminal activity. In other words, if Parker has already been up to any kind of shady shit, he has plenty of reasons to not want a PI poking around in his business, whether his son killed Caroline Duncan or not."

Jimmy listened to Howard's words and then frowned.

"None of this matters anyway," he said. "Even if there was a way to prove that Parker kid killed the girl, which there doesn't seem to be, you don't have time, Tracy. The sheriff has it out for you. And I'm not interested in hanging around in this shit hole long enough to join you. It's hot as hell, and the mosquitos are brutal."

She turned away from them and sat down on the bed. Howard winced as he watched her grimace with every movement, as if her body were some fragile thing made of glass.

"You did everything you could, Tracy," he said. "It's not your fault."

She sat for a moment and looked at the carpet.

"No," she said at last. "There's still one more thing I can do."

Howard and Jimmy traded looks.

"What?" asked the lawyer.

Tracy struggled to her feet.

"I'm going to talk to the sheriff."

Chapter 13

It was just after 11 p.m. when Tracy arrived outside the sheriff's office. High in the sky, the stars were lost to a thick matte of willowy clouds. Light thunder crackled in the heavens as flits of rain ticked and popped against the hot evening streets.

At the edge of the world, a big-bellied moon hung heavy and white where the clouds broke in the low horizon. Tracy looked at the glowing ball as the rain spattered her broken face. She took a deep breath and scanned the empty sidewalks. But there wasn't much to see. So, she limped up to the front door and made her way inside.

She found the sheriff sitting at his desk with a coffee cup and a small bottle of whiskey, which he tried to hide when he heard the sound of footsteps.

"Who's there?" he asked as he peered into the shadowed entryway.

Tracy stepped into the light and stood as he looked up at her and swallowed.

"Jesus," he said as he studied her swollen, discolored face. He half stood and then sat back down. He shook his head and swallowed.

"You look like you got run over by something."

She shrugged and winced a little.

"You should see the other guy."

He watched as she limped into the room.

"I did see the other guys," he said. "Or what was left of 'em. They're all laid up in the hospital. Look like they got run down by a semi. Two of them haven't even woke up yet."

She assumed a look of false concern.

"That's a shame."

He pushed his bottom lip out and leaned back in his chair.

You have anything to do with that?"

Tracy stifled a false laugh.

"I wish." She gestured to the seat across from his desk. "Mind if I sit?"

"Please," he said as he motioned toward it.

She sat down like an elderly woman, her teeth gritting while she lowered herself into the seat. He watched her with a deep frown.

"Well," he said. "Them boys have made their share of enemies. It was only a matter of time before someone came callin, I suppose."

She finally settled in her seat and sighed.

"Well, don't expect any tears from me."

He nodded.

"I suppose you're wondering why I haven't arrested them for the assault on you."

She shook her head.

"I'm not here about that."

He raised his eyebrows.

"No?"

"No," she said. "I'm here about Caroline Duncan."

He let out an exasperated sigh.

"Not this shit again. We've been over it. Why can't you let it go? It's caused nothing but trouble. And there ain't nothin left to look at."

She sat back in her seat and looked at him.

"Why are you so sure?"

"Because," he said. "These types of crimes are always domestic things. It's always a boyfriend or a husband. At least out here it is."

She shook her head.

"There's no murder weapon to tie her boyfriend to the crime. All you have is some witnesses that said he left the hotel long enough to have an opportunity. But there's no real motive. You've got a case that screams reasonable doubt. You should be happy for my help. If you have the right man, anything I find will only support that and make your job much easier."

He shook his head.

"A PI like you will only corrupt the case. You should know that from when you were a real cop. Anyway, there's nothing out here to find. This ain't like the city, where you got witnesses on every block. Out here, the only witnesses are the bugs and the bats and the owls. And the bodies don't leave clues cause half the time the gators get em."

She looked into his eyes.

"What about Silas Brown?"

He furrowed his eyebrows.

"What about him?"

She leaned forward in her chair.

"Caroline's brother said he lives near the scene of the crime. Maybe he saw something."

The sheriff shook his head.

"Nah."

Tracy raised her eyebrows.

"Did you talk to him?"

The sheriff shook his head.

"Nope."

"Why not?"

He rubbed his eyes and sighed, as if trying to reason with an imbecile.

"Cause he's bat-shit crazy. That's why. He don't talk to nobody. He's an old veteran. Got PTSD or some shit. Lives out in the deep woods by himself. I mean the deep, deep woods. He's a survivalist. Crazy as all hell. He ain't gonna talk to me or you or nobody willingly. He'd just as soon shoot you dead the moment you step onto his land. Anyway, even if you could get him to talk. And you couldn't, I promise you, his testimony wouldn't hold up."

"Why not?" asked Tracy.

"Cause he's insane, Ms. Sterling. And I don't mean quirky shit like touching the doorknob three times because of your OCD. I mean drinking his own piss and saving his fingernails in jars. That kind of crazy."

She raised her eyebrows.

"Why isn't he a suspect?"

"He's 90 years old," said the sheriff. "That girl's autopsy showed no drugs, no alcohol in her system. No bonk on the head.

Nothin that would allow a 90-year-old man to physically overpower her. Whoever killed that girl was fit as a fiddle. Not some loony-tunes hermit with arthritis and a bum hip. Anyway, for all I know, that old man's dead and rotting. Ain't nobody seen him in over a year."

She shrugged.

"I still want to talk to him."

He sighed.

"Didn't you hear what I said?"

"I'll take my chances," she said.

He shook his head.

"No, you won't. What you'll do is get in your car, you and your lawyer friend, and drive on out of here tonight. Or else I'm gonna arrest you for what you did to Beaux Parker's truck."

She narrowed her eyes at him.

"Is that what Bill Parker told you to do?"

His face flushed, and his eyes narrowed.

"Now, listen here—"

"No, you listen," said Tracy. "It's true. I haven't been able to find out much about this case. But I have uncovered a few things. So, let me tell you some stuff you may not know."

He started to speak, but she just spoke louder.

"Did you know Parker found rare earth minerals in his quarry?"

The sheriff shook his head.

"What difference does that make?"

"It makes a big difference for this town because it means he's going to sell the rights to a corporation, an outside corporation that won't give a damn about you or your town."

The sheriff frowned at this.

"I'm not following."

Tracy leaned closer and put a hand on his desk.

"These rare earth minerals are very valuable. They're critical for phones, computers, military technology. Everything that matters. They're worth billions. Not millions. Billions. But to mine them, they have to tear everything down. And when I say everything, sheriff, I mean everything. Including this whole fucking town."

He rubbed his jaw and looked at her.

"Bullshit."

She leaned forward and shook her head.

"Not bullshit. Once they start mining for these minerals, the water will be fouled. The land will be toxic. There won't be a town anymore because there can't be one. It'll all be torn down. The bar, the barbershop, you're fucking house. All of it, gone as soon as Bill Parker signs the deal."

He looked down at his desk and swallowed. Then, he got up and turned toward the window. She watched as he stared outside, where rain filled the puddles in the street.

"When is this happening?"

"I don't know," says Tracy. "But soon. And the only thing that might have a chance of stopping it is if something were to come to light. Some kind of information that Parker might want to keep hidden. Something that might turn off the buyer and blow the whole deal."

The sheriff stared out the window without speaking, his eyes focused on nothing as he considered her words.

"Sheriff," she said, her voice lower and softer than before. "I think Beaux Parker killed Caroline Duncan. He and his friends. I think they chased her through the woods and terrorized her. And maybe they didn't intend to, or maybe they did. Who knows? But whatever the case, in the end, things got out of control, and they drowned her in that pond."

She stopped talking and sat back in her chair. It was quiet except for the rain, which tapped against the window glass as faint thunder rumbled in the heavens.

"I can't do nothing for you, Ms. Sterling," he said without turning around. "I'm sorry. I just can't."

She shook her head.

"You don't need to do anything," she said. "Not really. "Just tell me how to find Silas Brown. I'll try to talk to him. If I learn something, great. If not, I'll be out of your hair."

He shook his head as he stared into the night.

"You won't find out nothin," he said. "There ain't no point.

He spoke in a quiet voice that made him seem older. Diminished.

It was quiet for a while. And then Tracy took a deep breath and spoke.

"Listen, Sheriff. My dad was a great cop. He won awards for his detective work. Solved some of the city's most unsolvable crimes. He was famous for it. And I idolized him. Everyone did. And I wanted to be just like him. He was a legend. He was revered. But you probably already know all that if you really read up on me, like you said. And you also probably also know that my dad wasn't really who he claimed to be."

The sheriff stood as before, his body still as he stared out the window.

"Now," Tracy continued. "One thing you wouldn't have read on the internet in all the news reports is that I found a letter he wrote shortly before he died. It was a confession to all his mistakes. But it was also more than that. It was filled with regret. And it broke my heart because I knew, I still know, that he was a good man on the inside. And I could tell in the words he wrote that he was shattered by the fact that it was too late to make things right."

The sheriff said nothing, and she squirmed a little in her seat as she tried to speak passionately to the back of his head.

"Now, I don't know your business, sheriff. And I can only guess about your history. But I look at you, and I think deep down inside, you're also a good man. And I think all these years, even if you don't know it, I think all these years, you've been waiting. Waiting for a chance to make things right. Well, here I am, Sheriff. Here I am with your chance. Are you going to take it? Or are you going to sit alone in an empty house and write a sad, pointless letter before you die?"

He kept staring outside, his demeanor unchanged. And for a moment, she actually thought about turning to run.

"Why do you think that old man can tell you anything?" he said without turning around.

She hesitated for a moment, and then the words came spilling out.

"The other night, when I was out there in the woods, I was in and out of consciousness most the night. I don't remember a lot, but I do remember seeing something."

He turned slightly without looking at her.

"What?"

She took a deep breath, her eyes watching him intently as she spoke.

"A little box strapped to a tree."

He frowned at this.

"A box?"

She nodded.

"A little camouflage box with a camera on it."

He turned around.

"A trail cam?"

116

She nodded.

"I've asked around," she said. "Most people won't talk to me, but some do. Some are lonely. The old ones, mostly. They're just glad to have someone to talk to. And a few of them told me Silas Brown puts these trail cams up all over. And not just to watch animals either. And also not just on his land."

The sheriff sat back down in his chair and clasped his hands together. He stared down at the desk for a few moments. Then, he retrieved the whiskey bottle from under his desk. She watched as he unscrewed the cap and filled the cup halfway. He sighed and drank the whole thing down. Then, he hissed inward and looked at her.

"If I allow this," he said. "It'll be under specific terms."

"Such as?" she asked.

"Such as, if you find any relevant, compelling evidence, you immediately bring it to me. And if not, you leave town tomorrow morning, no questions asked."

She studied him for a moment.

"What will you do if I bring you the evidence?"

He glared at her.

"If you bring me evidence of a crime, I'll arrest the perpetrator."

She raised her eyebrows.

"Even if it's Beaux Parker?"

He nodded slowly.

"Yes."

She nodded.

"You got a deal."

He shook his head and withdrew a sheet of paper from his desk.

"This place is hard to find," he said as he started to sketch a little map. "You can't drive right up to it."

She waited for him to finish and then took the paper from his hand.

"You should know," he said. "There's a real chance he might just shoot you on sight."

She nodded.

"How about you give me my gun, then?"

He shook his head.

"The last thing I need is a shootout between a New York PI and a geriatric local. No, ma'am. If you're gonna pull this off, it's gonna

117

have to be with your words. And that's if he's still alive. And I'm not exaggerating when I say you may very well find him dead in a rocking chair."

She nodded.

"Fine."

He sat back in his chair and raised his eyebrows.

"You'd better get started."

She pinched her eyebrows together.

"What? Tonight?"

He nodded.

That's right."

"Sheriff, you really think it's best for me to just charge onto this guy's land in the middle of the night? Why not give me until tomorrow morning?"

He shook his head.

"Bill Parker is gonna be in this office tomorrow morning. He's gonna insist that I arrest you for what happened to his son. And if I refuse, he'll insist that I at least arrest you for shooting out his tires the other day. My hands will be tied unless you've already left town. So, it's tonight or never. Make your decision, Ms. Sterling."

She sighed and stood up.

"Fine," she said. "I'll go tonight."

He looked up at her.

"Alright, then. As long as we understand each other. You've got tonight. That's all. You're gone in the morning, no matter what. Is that clear?"

She nodded and turned for the door.

"Ms. Sterling," said the sheriff as she reached for the door.

Tracy turned.

"You might want to rethink this. Nobody goes out to that place. And I mean nobody. I went one time back when I first got this job. And one time was enough for me. If that old fucker's still around, he won't be happy to see you. Especially this time of night."

Tracy nodded.

"Thanks for the advice."

He gave her a little nod. And then he stood up and watched her through the window as she crossed the street and vanished down the road.

Chapter 14

Tracy squeezed the steering wheel as they pushed deep into the swampy landscape. The barren road curved sharply as it cut a path through the endless miles of marshy terrain, which almost seemed to glow under the color of the big pale moon.

Jimmy glanced at her from the passenger seat.

"Ease up, will you? I don't want to end up out here in a ditch."

Tracy shook her head, her one open eye wide as she watched for crossing wildlife.

"We're short on time."

Jimmy looked out the window, where a black wall of trees whirred past.

"Are you sure you know where we're going?"

She nodded.

"The sheriff said there's a pull-off a few miles up ahead. From there, we walk."

He sighed.

"Wonderful."

She shook her head and stared forward, where the headlights carved a pathway into the infinite darkness. On both sides of the road, trees stretched on indefinitely, their branches heavy with draping Spanish moss. Behind them, the swamp loomed dark and deep, and she shuddered on the inside as she remembered her night in the wild.

As they crested a small hill, the trees cleared on one side, and a marshy body of water appeared in the near distance. Tracy pointed across the cattails and reeds toward the big marshy pond, which shone like onyx glass under the light of the bleached moon.

"The sheriff said the pull-off area is about a mile past that water."

Sure enough, they spotted a dusty pull-off area a little further down the road. Tracy slowed the vehicle and turned onto the uneven ground, the vehicle jolting as the tires bumped over the rutted earth. When she stopped the car, the headlights revealed a narrow, underused trail that burrowed into the heart of the swampland. She looked at Jimmy with a furrowed brow.

"I guess that's it."

He looked through the windshield and frowned at the tunneling path.

"I don't know why I agreed to this," he said as he opened the door.

She started to speak, but he had already stepped out into the hot night. Taking a deep breath, she grabbed her flashlight and opened her door to join him.

Outside, the humid air smelled of damp earth and cypress. She scanned the area and listened, but there wasn't much to see or hear. So, she flicked on her flashlight with a sharp click that seemed to explode in the quiet night.

Jimmy removed his pistol and levered a bullet into the chamber. He reholstered the weapon and removed his own flashlight.

"Well," he said. "Let's get on with it."

They turned towards the ragged dirt trail, which split a patch of tall marsh grasses as it snaked away from the small pull-off area. Jimmy switched on his flashlight and illuminated the narrow footpath, where it plunged into the dense thicket. Tracy took his arm as he stepped forward.

"Stay on the trail," she said. "It really is a swamp out here. The land turns to water without warning. You'll be waste-deep before you know it."

He looked at her bruised and battered face.

"Well," he said. "I suppose you would know."

He turned away and pushed into the thicket, his large form vanishing as it swallowed him whole. Tracy hurried to catch up, her flashlight cutting thick, laser-like beams into the swallowing night. A light, wispy fog had begun to roll out from the marshy bog waters, and now it tumbled over the trail like smoke from some unseen fire.

Over the years, nature had reclaimed the old trail, and they ducked and dodged limbs, like tense partygoers in some peculiar game of limbo dreamt up by a madman's brain. One of the branches slapped Jimmy in the face, and he paused and clutched his stinging nose.

"Shit," he hissed.

They paused and waited. All around, the cypress trees groaned as a light breeze pushed their big branches, which clattered with a ghostly racket out in the darkness. Something big scurried through the brush and then plunged with an audible gloomp into a shallow body of water.

"Listen," Tracy said as she sprayed her flashlight into the woods. "Did you hear that?"

Jimmy paused and strained to hear, but it was quiet except for Tracy's nose, which whistled like a tiny teakettle with every breath.

"I can't hear anything over your nose," he said.

"What?" she asked as she turned toward him.

He frowned down at her, his hard features lost to the darkness.

"I can hear your nose whistling. So can anyone else."

She glared at him.

"It's broken, Jimmy. What am I supposed to do?"

"You can breathe through your mouth."

She put a hand on her hip.

"I am breathing through my mouth."

"Then, why can I hear your nose?"

She sighed.

"There's nothing I can do about it, Jimmy. It's broken."

"Here," he said as he reached a hand out.

Before she could pull away, he had her nose between his thumb and index finger. With a quick twist, he gave it a crack. Her eyes poured water as the pain knifed through her skull.

"What the fuck!" she shrieked in a hissing whisper of a voice.

"Relax," he said. "Try now."

She glared up into his face with brazen hate. Then, she took a breath, and the air came in and out cleanly and quietly through her nostrils.

"Holy shit," she said as she brought a hand to her face. "How did you do that?"

He shrugged.

121

"Don't thank me," he said. "It'll hurt like a bitch tomorrow."

With that, he turned and proceeded up the trail. Tracy frowned at his words and rubbed her nose. She looked around and followed him up the path.

All around them, crickets chirped out in the endless black. Somewhere in the distance, a low hoot pierced the night as an owl announced its presence.

On they walked, their shoes squelching as they moved through intermittent puddles of water that had gathered up in little cavities throughout the trail. All the while, Tracy scanned their flanks with the flashlight, while gnats and mosquitos fluttered in and out of the beam, their iridescent wings sparkling briefly and then vanishing into the darkness once more.

As they walked, she heard the occasional rustle out in the marshy darkness as unseen creatures went about their nocturnal lives. Somewhere in the distance, an alligator's low growl rumbled across the water, and she felt her heart stick in her throat.

"Hold up," said Jimmy as he shined his flashlight in the path.

Tracy's eyes followed his gaze to the carpet of leaves that lay before them.

"What?" she said.

He pointed a few feet in front of them.

"There."

She looked at the spot and shook her head.

"It's just a lot of dead leaves."

He looked at her.

"In the middle of summer?"

Tracy looked back at the stretch of trail and narrowed her eyes. Now, she could see it. The path looked softer and subtly different from its surroundings. She turned and watched as Jimmy approached a tree and tore away a considerable branch. The thing came away with a sharp crack, and she winced as something large scurried amid the brush out in the lightless woods.

"Stand back," he said.

He approached with the big branch and tossed it onto the leaves a few feet before them. As if swallowed up by a great hidden mouth, the entire thing vanished into the earth as a hole opened up around it. Tracy looked at him.

"What the hell?"

He shook his head.

122

"It's a punji pit."

"A what?" she asked.

Jimmy shook his head.

"A pitfall covered in mesh and leaves. There are probably spikes at the bottom."

They approached with creeping footsteps. As they neared the edge, Jimmy shined his light down into the large hole. Sure enough, the bottom was barbed with rows of sharpened metal spikes that winked ominously in the light.

"Jesus," said Tracy.

Jimmy sighed and looked all around.

"You sure about this?" he asked.

She looked down into the floor of the pit, which seemed to move as centipedes and grub larvae wiggled amid the long rusty spikes.

"Yes."

Jimmy withdrew his pistol.

"Stay close," he said. "This guy's obviously as crazy as they say. And if there's one of these, there are probably more. And maybe other little surprises as well. We need to take it very, very slow. My eyes aren't what they used to be, so keep an eye out for tripwires. And watch the trees, so we don't walk right under a big log or some other bullshit."

She sighed and nodded.

"Right."

He looked at her and frowned.

"I want a nice cut of whatever Howard's paying you for this thing."

She nodded.

"Yeah."

He turned and gripped his pistol.

"Let's go."

Carefully, they edged around the yawning pit and moved further along the trail. With painstaking care, they proceeded, wide eyes darting about as they crept on their toes, like soldiers navigating a battlefield laced with hidden mines.

About 100 feet further, they found a second pitfall and deftly maneuvered around it without springing the trap. Then, shortly after, they came upon a pair of big metal, bear snap-traps, which sat obvious and unhidden in the middle of the trail.

Tracy paused and looked around. She grabbed Jimmy's arm and leaned in to whisper.

"Why leave these here unconcealed?"

"Who knows?" he said. "Maybe they're here to catch someone running. Or maybe they're just distractions from the real traps. Whatever the case, I am seriously considering kicking this guy's ass when I find him."

He searched the ground for a pair of sticks and used them to spring the two traps. The jaws snapped at the empty air with a sickening crunch that made Tracy imagine splintering shin bones.

"Let's go," said Jimmy.

Onward they crept, their movements laced with a heightened sense of dread, each and every step carrying the weight of potential doom. A lapse in caution meant death, or at bare minimum, a gruesome maiming, so they moved in silent agreement to regard the world with strained attention.

By the time they saw the old house looming in the little clearing, they'd encountered two more bear traps and a third pitfall. Tracy clutched her fractured ribs as they stood amid the dark edges of the treeline.

"You alright?" asked Jimmy.

She nodded.

"I'll make it."

They turned and regarded the house before them. Perched upon a gentle slope, the two-story structure loomed with a crooked slant amid the swaying trees. All the years of hot, moist air had bent the old gray dwelling, warping it into a sort of twisted, funhouse-like geometry that made an eerie silhouette beneath the ghostly lunar glow.

Jimmy shook his head.

"That cut I asked for?"

She looked up at him.

"Make it a big one," he said.

She nodded.

"Absolutely."

They crossed a lawn of overgrown swamp grass, every footstep slow and careful as they watched for traps. When they approached the structure, their eyes turned to the windows, which were all broken and lightless.

"This place looks abandoned," whispered Tracy.

Jimmy nodded.

"Or maybe he really is dead."

Tracy frowned at this.

"Let's check it out."

They reached the porch of the house, which sat atop a three-step rise, its old wood warped and gray.

"Look," whispered Tracy.

Jimmy nodded as his eyes moved to the front door, which was open about three inches.

"I see it," he said.

They studied every inch of the rotting platform, their eyes meticulous as they searched for traps. But it was just an old porch. So, they stepped onto it and approached the front door. Jimmy took a step back and raised his pistol, while Tracy balled up her fist to knock.

"Mr. Brown," she called as she rapped her knuckles against the wood.

The door groaned as it fell open a few more inches. They waited, but there was no response.

"Mr. Brown," she called through the open gap. "We're not here to bother you. We'd just like to ask you a couple of questions, if that's alright."

They waited, but the old man did not return her call. Tracy looked back at Jimmy, who shrugged. She turned and knocked again, and the door opened another couple of inches. Now, the moonlight knifed into the gap well enough to illuminate the toe of a boot amid the impenetrable shadows at the other side of the room.

"Mr. Brown?" called Tracy as she pushed the door open.

"Wait!" called Jimmy.

His hand closed around the back of her shirt, and she felt herself being yanked backward as a whir of metal came flashing at her face. There was a wooshing sound and then a clank of metal on wood, and then it was still except for the beating of her heart.

"What the fuck is that?" she asked.

A small log hung vertically in the doorway. At its tip, there was a metal spike that jutted forth in the space where Tracy had been standing.

"It's some sort of pendulum trap," Jimmy said as he shook his head. "He attached it to the ceiling. When you open the door, it comes swinging down and guts you on the welcome mat."

She approached and looked over. The blade was at least six inches long and sharp enough to split bone.

"My God," she whispered.

Jimmy nodded and pushed against the log, which now blocked entry to the home.

"Guess we need to find another way in," he said.

"Hold on," said Tracy.

She approached the entryway and shined her light into the house. Inside, there was a large empty room with a few wooden crates, a stack of old newspapers, and at the far side, against a wall, there sat a pair of old empty boots. She shook her head.

"Ok. Let's go."

They moved off the porch and made their way to the side of the house. There was a single window that was still intact, despite a dense webbing of hairline cracks. They approached it cautiously, their eyes searching the ground and the air and even the treeline behind them.

When they reached the window, Jimmy raised his gun and shined the light inside.

"What do you see?" asked Tracy.

"Not much," he said. "Garbage and boxes. It doesn't look like anyone lives here anymore. I think this is a dead end. Maybe we should forget it."

The feeling had returned to Tracy's nose, and she rubbed it and grimaced.

"No," she said. "Let's find out for sure."

He sighed and gave her the gun and the flashlight.

"Here. Hold these."

She shined the light while he wrenched up the window, which didn't even appear to have a lock. The thing gave way with a piercing shriek as the swollen wood edges raked against the frame. They paused and looked around while the noise echoed into the night.

"Hand me the light," said Jimmy.

She passed it over, and he illuminated the interior. It was a small bedroom that looked ill-suited for even the tiniest bed. The door was shut, the floor was littered with trash and cardboard, and the odor in the room was as stale as stale could possibly be.

"Delightful," he said flatly as he passed the flashlight back to Tracy.

She watched as he swung a leg into the opening and straddled the windowsill. He lifted his body up and pushed into the house. He searched the floor for footing and brought his boot down hard. Tracy flinched as he inhaled sharply.

"What's wrong?" she asked. "She shone the light on his face and saw that he was grimacing with pain.

"My foot," he whispered through gritting teeth. She leaned in past him and lit the floor.

"Oh, shit," she whispered.

The old man had hammered several dozen long nails through a thin plywood board and placed it beneath the window. Jimmy had stepped right onto the makeshift trap, and now his foot was impaled by at least three nails. One had come through the top near his toes, and its tip glinted in the light as blood boiled up and out of the boot.

Tracy shook her head.

"You're gonna have to pull it off."

He cursed as she stepped back. Then, he bit his lip and jerked his knee upward. A tiny shriek escaped his lips as his foot came free.

Tracy watched as he fell backward out of the window and onto the grass. He cursed again as he pushed himself up against the house. He shook his head and flexed his toes. She shined her light on his boot and winced as blood oozed from the holes.

"Should we take it off?"

He shook his head.

"I'll never get it back on."

He gritted his teeth and held out a hand. She took it and helped him onto his feet.

"If this old fucker is still alive, I'm gonna kill him," he said.

Tracy started to speak but stopped at the sound of footsteps coming from inside the house.

"Shh," she said to Jimmy, who didn't seem to have noticed anything except the pain in his wounded foot.

He winced a little and strained to listen.

"What?" he asked.

"I heard footsteps inside the house," she said. "Just on the other side of that bedroom door."

"You sure?"

She nodded.

Jimmy sighed and approached the window, his face straining with every limping step. He shone the light inside at the closed door. Then, he lit the floor and shook his head at all the rows of nails popping up from the plywood.

"How do we get over it?" asked Tracy.

Jimmy assessed the nails thoughtfully.

127

"'We' don't do shit. 'You' pile enough dirt and rocks on it, so we can walk over it, while I sit and rest."

She watched as he sat down. Then, she fell to her knees and started clawing her fingers against the earth.

In about ten minutes, she had buried enough of the board with rocks and dirt to cover the nails and support their weight. Slowly, they both climbed through the window and onto the rocks. Then, they stepped out onto the floor of the little bedroom.

The wood creaked as they found their footing, and Tracy watched as Jimmy bent down and hooked his hand beneath the plywood. With a mighty heave, he tossed it over away from the window so the nails pointed down against the floor.

"In case we need to come back this way in a hurry," he muttered.

She nodded.

"Let's go."

She watched as he limped, her face wincing as his boot stamped the creaking wood floor with bloody red imprints.

"Maybe you should have waited outside."

He shook his head and flexed his jaw.

"I'll be fine. Anyway, I'd like to have a word with this guy."

She gave his boot a doubtful look and followed him to the door.

"How do you want to do this?" she asked.

When I open the door, take a step back and shine the light. She watched as he raised his gun and moved toward the door. She grabbed his arm, and he paused.

"Don't shoot him, Jimmy. This is technically a home invasion at this point."

He nodded.

"Just hold the light."

Without another word, he raised his gun and pulled open the door. With a sweeping movement, Tracy illuminated a dark hallway, while Jimmy darted his pistol around.

"It's clear," he said. "Let's go."

He limped forward, and his foot came down on a loose floorboard. There was a faint metallic click as the board gave way about an inch. An acrid chemical smell flooded the hallway as a cloud of blue dust exploded around him. Tracy stumbled backward and coughed, her eyes squinting as the dust wafted in the air.

"Jimmy!"

She watched as he slowly turned around, his face and body coated in blue dye.

"Are you alright?" she asked.

He glared at her, his eyes afire as they stared out from his bright blue face. He looked like some sort of sadistic smurf-like figure. And she nearly had to stifle a laugh as he sneered his impossibly white teeth at her.

"Not a word."

She approached and touched his face. She brought her fingers back and rubbed them together.

"It's explosive dye, like the kind banks use. There must be a pressure plate under this board." She looked up at him. "There could be more. And it may be worse than dye. Let's slow down."

He scowled at her, and they moved down the hallway.

"Mr. Brown," she called out as they crept forward. "If you can hear us, we're not here to hurt you. We just want to ask you a couple of questions."

They crept down the hallway, their toes lightly testing each warped board in advance before delivering their full weight. When they reached the end of the hall, they paused and looked at each other. Then, like a single, unified entity, they spun around the corner, Jimmy's gun up and darting around, while Tracy cast the room in light.

In the corner, a small, bearded figure stood, his body frail and malnourished, bright eyes watching them from within a riot of gray, unwashed hair. Tracy started to speak, but the man tossed something onto the floor in front of them. A deafening bang echoed in the confined space, as a flash bang lit the room like a tiny sun. They slammed their eyelids shut and staggered backward, dazzling spots dancing in their vision as they tried to shake off the disorienting effects.

Through the white haze of blindness and shock, Tracy saw a fleeting shadow dart across the room, a mere specter in the chaotic darkness. The figure darted into the adjacent room, slamming the door behind him with a sharp echo.

Cursing, Jimmy stormed across the room and reached for the doorknob, his hand wrapping around it firmly. But instead of the expected cold metal, a surge of electricity snapped at his hand, and his body jolted, convulsing as he crashed onto the floor.

"Jimmy!" cried Tracy as she stumbled toward him.

He writhed and coughed.

129

"Just go," he hissed as he handed her his gun.

She stood up and approached the door. With a swift, forceful kick, she hammered her shoe just beneath the doorknob, and the thing came open like a swinging gate. She raised her gun and blinked, her eyes streaked with sun dazzles as she shined her light into the dark room. A figure cowered in the corner, his body curled in a defensive posture.

"Mr. Brown," said Tracy as she approached. "Please relax. We're not here to hurt you."

With his wild beard, the reclusive hermit looked every bit the mountain man. And as Tracy approached, he darted his head from left to right, like a small rodent looking for a way around a predator. As she crept forward, Tracy's eyes began to clear, and she used them to assess the man and the room for any hidden dangers. But there was only more garbage, and more newspapers, save for a five-gallon bucket and a bottle of bleach, which the old man cradled like a frightened child clutching an old Teddy bear.

Tracy slipped the pistol into her belt and eased closer, her hand out as if she were attempting to soothe a wild animal.

"It's alright," she said in a gentle whisper of a voice. "Everything's alright."

The old man regarded her with wide, hazy eyes, his breathing ragged, body tense. She opened her mouth to speak again, when stomping boots filled the space behind her. She turned to see Jimmy entering the room, his big blue body swelling up as he barged forward with hate in his eyes.

"Hold on, Jimmy," said Tracy.

The old man flinched a little, and then turned the bottle of bleach upside down over the five-gallon bucket. In an instant, the smell of vinegar and chlorine flooded the room. Tracy stepped back and coughed as the old man climbed to his feet. Like a much younger man, he bolted between them on his way to the open door. On instinct, Jimmy reached out to grab the man's arm, but he snatched only air as the twisted hermit escaped the room and slammed the door shut behind him.

Jimmy limped to the door and turned the knob.

"Locked," he said.

He clutched his burning chest and coughed.

"What is that?"

Tracy wheezed and spat.

130

"Chlorine gas. He mixed vinegar and bleach."

Enveloped in the noxious cloud, they banged away at the door, their lungs screaming for fresh air as tears rained from their stinging eyes.

"Stand back," Jimmy gasped as he raised his bad leg.

With a grimace, he slammed his bloody boot against the door over and over, the world beginning to spin as his head grew faint.

At last, there was a great crack, and the hinges began to give way. With one last bloody stomp, he sent the entire thing flying off its frame, and they burst out of the toxic cloud. Wheezing and gasping, they collapsed onto the floor, their lungs pulling for air as they tugged the collars from their burning throats.

They stared at the ceiling and coughed, their eyes blinking as tears streamed down their cheeks.

"Ok," Tracy finally whispered in a hoarse voice. "You can kill him."

Jimmy coughed and turned his head to spit. Then, he struggled to his feet and reached out a hand. Tracy took it and pulled herself up. She bent over and tried to restrain vomit, while Jimmy found his flashlight and lit up the room. At the far end, behind some old boxes, a rickety flight of stairs pushed down into a basement.

Jimmy spat, and his saliva came out blue. He shook his head.

"Come on."

Tracy followed him to the top of the stairs. He shined the light and shook his head. There were about eight wood steps, and all of them looked ready to buckle, save for one around the middle that looked brand new. Jimmy frowned at it.

"Step on it or step over it?" asked Tracy.

He thought for a moment.

"Your call."

She rubbed her nose, which now stung with every breath.

"Over it."

He nodded and gestured toward her.

"Gun."

She handed it over, and they descended.

With each step, the wood groaned its complaints, and their pores bled sweat as they waited for some terrible outcome. An explosion, perhaps or a collapsing step. Maybe darts tipped with poison or a falling net. And all the while, they kept their eyes glued to the

131

door, Jimmy's pistol up and waiting in case the old man yanked it open to spray them with gunfire.

But nothing came, and once they stepped over the new wood, they arrived at the concrete landing in a few quick steps, their hearts throbbing as they paused to catch their breath.

"Ready?" asked Jimmy without looking back.

"Yes."

Without another word, he rammed his shoulder into the door and smashed into the room on the other side. Bright light stung his eyes, and he squinted as he aimed his gun in every direction. The old man stood in the corner, his hands up as he retreated against a wall.

"Sit," said Jimmy as he aimed his gun.

The old man sneered at him as he retreated back into the corner and crouched down against the wall. Tracy entered the room and looked around. Overhead, flickering fluorescent lights cast long, stuttering shadows over the surrounding concrete walls, which were shelved with boxes of loose canned goods.

To the right, a pair of old security monitors flickered with ghostly gray static. Positioned next to them sat an old-style PC computer, its big boxy hard drive gently whirring amid the quiet.

Around the monitors, maps were scattered, their features dotted with tiny markings and symbols she could not understand. Next to these sat an old short-wave radio, along with a stack of survival guides, along with military strategy books and classic dystopian novels.

Her eyes traveled to the old man, who crouched low next to a green canvas cot and a small propane stove. He stared at her with his feral eyes. Then, her eyes traveled to his hands.

"Jimmy," she whispered.

Within his long, almost skeletal fingers, the man held what appeared to be a very-old looking grenade. He stared at one and then the other, his pale gray eyes laced with pure hate.

"Get out," he spat.

Jimmy flexed his jaw and gripped his pistol.

"Just relax."

The old man reached for the pin and roared.

"Get out!"

Tracy put a hand on Jimmy's shoulder and then looked at the old man.

"Mr. Brown," she started. "Can I call you Silas?"

He glared at her and showed his yellow teeth.

I'm warning you," he said, his coarse voice grated by age. "Get out, or I'll blow you both to hell."

Jimmy raised his eyebrows.

"And yourself."

The old man's eyes flicked over, and his mouth bent into a madman's grin.

"Death is but a doorway."

Tracy took Jimmy's arm and squeezed.

"Silas," she said. "We're not here to cause any trouble. This is your home, and we should not be here."

He looked at her and narrowed his eyes. She took a step toward him, her hands up in surrender.

"We wouldn't have come. But we are desperate. And we need your help."

He regarded her with suspicious intensity. But his hand fell away from the pin of the explosive.

"You're trying to trick me."

"No," she said as she offered a kind smile.

She took another step forward, and he pressed his back against the wall, his hand returning to the pin as he took in several quick breaths.

Jimmy gripped his pistol and chewed his teeth. Tracy paused and held her hands up.

"I'm sorry," she said. "I didn't mean to startle you."

"Stay back," he hissed.

She nodded.

"Listen, Silas. A young girl was killed not far from here, and we're trying to find the person who did it. We know you have trail cams out here. We'd like to take a look at any footage you might have collected the night of the crime."

He sneered up at her.

"Get out!"

Tracy sighed and pointed at his computer.

"You might have video of the killer right there. Please just let us take a look."

The old man shook his head and clutched the explosive like it was the only thing he had left in the world.

"It's mine," he said as he flashed his rotting teeth. "You can't have it!"

Tracy looked at him and shook her head.

133

"Please, sir. This is evidence of a murder. Don't you want justice for this girl?

He raised his upper lip as if to growl.

"What I want is you off my property."

Jimmy shook his head.

"Oh, for Christ's sake. What if we give you some money?"

The old man looked up at him. He sniffed the air and sucked his cheek a little. Then, he raised his bushy eyebrows and pushed his bottom lip out.

"How much?"

Chapter 15

They were all waiting for Tracy when she stepped into the sheriff's office early in the morning. She heard their voices long before she opened the door. So, she paused to listen before stepping into view.

Bill Parker was talking to—or more accurately—at the sheriff, his southern accent thicker than ever as he chastised the lawman for this and that. He wasn't asking questions. He was giving orders. And something about that made Tracy want to turn around and walk away.

"I think that's her," said the sheriff in a meek voice.

Tracy sighed and turned the corner.

All but one stood as she entered the room, the sheriff, Bill Parker, and a pair of his biggest men. But not Beaux. He did not stand. Instead, he sulked in his wheelchair, his two broken legs sealed up in big white casts that ran all the way down to his feet.

Tracy looked him over while they all stood in silence. The young man's head was wrapped in bandages that concealed his hair. His head was grotesquely lopsided with swelling flesh. And his face was colored by what seemed like one immense bruise.

His mouth gaped open as he breathed wetly. There was a black gap where one tooth used to be and a stitched tear that ran vertically from his bottom lip to his chin.

Drool leaked from his mouth as he regarded her with a mixture of hate and fear. Bill Parker followed Tracy's eyes to her son and gestured to one of his men. The big man removed a handkerchief from his pocket and dobbed at Beaux's slobber. Tracy moved her eyes to the other men and smiled.

"Oh, good," she said. "Everyone's here."

Bill Parker pointed at her.

"I want her arrested right now."

The sheriff frowned.

"What for, Bill?"

He turned toward the sheriff and put a hand on his hip.

"Well, let's start with the fact that my boy here is a veritable cripple."

The sheriff shrugged.

"I'm not following."

"God damn it, Sheriff, you know she had something to do with it. She may not have done it herself, but she knows the man who did."

The sheriff shook his head.

"Do you have any evidence to support that claim?"

Parker glared at him and raised his upper lip to show his teeth.

"Don't test me, Sheriff."

Tracy cleared her throat.

"I don't mean to interrupt. But as long as we're talking about evidence…"

They all watched as she slipped a small USB flash drive from her pocket.

"And what in the hell is that supposed to be?" asked the elder Parker.

Tracy raised her eyebrows.

"This? Oh, just some trail cam footage."

They all stared at her.

"Trail cam footage," Parker repeated flatly. He looked at the sheriff. "What the hell is she talking about?"

The sheriff looked at Tracy.

"Ms. Sterling, I'd recommend you start talking a little faster."

She nodded.

"Sure." She held the little flash drive up. "I was able to acquire this from Silas Brown last night. It holds footage from one of the many trail cams he has installed across a considerable expanse of land all around his property."

She looked at Beaux, and he swallowed.

"Sheriff—" Bill Parker started.

136

The sheriff held up his hand.

"What does this footage show, Ms. Sterling?"

She firmed her mouth.

"Why don't you see for yourself?"

She took a step forward and held it out. The sheriff swallowed and looked at her hand without moving. Bill Parker glanced at his son and showed his teeth a little.

"Now, hold on just a second," he said. "Sheriff, you need to think long and hard about your next move. Your career may depend on it. Your career, at least."

The sheriff took a deep breath and looked up at Tracy. She stared at him with her one good eye, which sank in hard and deep as his face took on a sheepish expression.

"What's on it?" he asked.

She shrugged.

"The truth. If you're man enough to see it."

He frowned at her. He approached and snatched it from her hand.

"Now, hold on," said Parker.

"Just sit tight, Bill," said the sheriff.

He walked over to his desk and opened a little laptop computer. They watched as he spun it around and inserted the flash drive.

"What am I looking for?" he asked.

Tracy looked over at Beaux, who was now studying the floor.

"This would be video footage from the night of Caroline Duncan's murder," she said. "You'll want to fast forward to just after 5:30 a.m."

He opened the file and expanded the video until it spanned the entire screen. The video showed black and white footage of a long trail that led from a thick, brambly wall of woods up to an old wood dock at the edge of a pond.

The sheriff sighed and looked back over his shoulder. Bill Parker's eyes moved from his son to Tracy to the sheriff and finally to the footage on the screen.

"Turn that off," he said. "Right now."

The sheriff took a deep breath.

"You hear me, Sheriff?" said Parker. "I said right now."

Tracy watched as the sheriff shook his head.

"You just sit tight and be quiet for a minute, Bill."

137

They all watched as the sheriff advanced the footage several hours until just before dawn. Then, something moved into the frame, and he let the video play.

They all watched in silence as Caroline Duncan staggered from the woods and limped blindly toward the edge of the pond, her feet tripping over the ground as she moved from left to right across the screen, where she stepped onto the dock and vanished out of sight.

They held their breath and waited for a few beats of a heart. And then, the sheriff shook his head as Beaux Parker emerged from the woods and followed Caroline onto the dock.

"Christ," the sheriff whispered.

Bill Parker looked down at his son with disgust. Then, his eyes traveled to Tracy, and his face colored with rage.

"This don't prove nothin," he said.

Tracy stifled laughter.

"No?" she said. She turned toward the sheriff. "What do you think?"

They watched as the sheriff turned around from the computer screen. His eyes studied the floor for a moment, while his jaw flexed noticeably under his old, leathery skin. And then he brought a hand to his belt. He removed a pair of handcuffs and looked at Beaux. '

"Beaux Parker, you're under arrest for the murder of Caroline Duncan."

Bill Parker's face took on a deeper shade of red, and Tracy half-expected steam to shoot from his ears.

"What are you doing?" he demanded.

"Quiet, Bill," said the sheriff. "Your boy is caught. It's all right there. The state DA probably already has a copy of this footage in his office."

Parker looked at his hulking men, but they only looked back like a pair of bewildered giants. The sheriff continued reading Beaux his rights, while the young man wept like a child.

"You," said Bill Parker as he pointed toward Tracy. "This isn't over. Not by a long shot. You messed with the wrong person. You made a very powerful enemy."

Tracy shrugged.

"That line starts at the back. Anyway, I think you may have your hands full for a little while. Silas Brown was a bit of a hoarder when it came to his trail cam footage. And some of those videos had other interesting stuff on them. Stuff like illegal dumping of chemicals and waste in the local waterways."

Parker froze, and the color ran from his face. Tracy raised her eyebrows.

"I went ahead and forwarded copies of all the relevant footage to the EPA and the South Carolina Department of Health and Environmental Control. I'm sure you'll be hearing from them soon."

She raised her eyebrows and looked over at Beaux, whose left hand was awkwardly cuffed to his right wrist, which draped over his chest in a sling.

"Well," she said with a friendly smile. "Thanks for the laughs."

With that, she turned and walked out the door, while Bill Parker watched in mute consternation, his mouth opening and closing slightly like a fish upon land. And he continued to stare at the empty space in the doorway long after she'd left the building, even while Beaux's sobbing filled the room.

Outside, the air was hot and heavy, but its weight fell like feathers on Tracy's upright shoulders. The moon bathed the street in an eerie glow that might have filled her with dread on any other night. But on this evening, it merely lit the way as she approached Howard and Jimmy with a smile.

The lawyer stood by the car, his head bowed a little as he spoke to Jimmy, who sat in the passenger seat, his face still stained blue and looking very tired.

"Well?" asked Howard as she approached.

She smiled.

"He's in cuffs."

Howard grinned.

"He'll be in worse soon. I emailed everything to the state DA. By morning, he'll be dropping the charges against Peter Teller and charging Beaux Parker. In a few hours, he'll be on his way to the Charleston jail to stand trial."

Tracy nodded and looked at Jimmy.

"Or maybe a Charleston hospital first."

Jimmy grimaced and rubbed at his foot, which was heavily wrapped in big white bandages.

"Let's get the fuck out of this shithole," he said. "Before we all end up in cuffs."

Howard nodded.

"That's a good idea," Howard said as he looked at Tracy. "There's a chance Jimmy could be recognized by Beaux Parker or his friends. And you've still got an open assault case here."

Tracy nodded.

"You don't have to ask me twice. I never want to see this place again."

Howard raised his eyebrows.

"I have a ticket for you waiting at the airport."

She shook her head.

"Thanks, but I'll drive him home." She looked at Jimmy. "That foot looks pretty bad. And it's the least I can do."

Jimmy grunted and looked away.

"Well," said Howard as he stuck out his hand. "I'll have a check sent out to you on Monday. You were worth every penny."

She took his hand and gave it a shake.

"Send half to my grumpy friend here."

Howard nodded.

"Sure thing."

He turned as if to leave and then paused a moment. He looked at Tracy and raised his eyebrows.

"You did it, Tracy. I tried to talk you out of it. But you got justice."

She shrugged.

"You were right though, Howard. What you said in the hotel. Ultimately, it's like trying to empty the ocean with a teaspoon. It's impossible in the end."

He shook his head.

"No," he said. "We just need more people to grab a spoon."

He looked at Jimmy and gave a little nod. "Jimmy."

Jimmy nodded back.

"Howard."

With that, he turned and walked away. They watched him stroll down the street toward his car, his posture tall and upright as he whistled a little tune. Tracy sighed and walked around to the driver's side of the vehicle. She opened the door and sat down.

"Keys," she said.

Jimmy handed them over.

"What kind of music am I going to be subjected to on this drive?" he asked.

She started the engine and put the car in reverse.

140

"Oh, a little smooth jazz. I've also been really into techno-pop lately."

He shook his head.

"Very funny."

She looked at him and smiled.

"I owe you, Jimmy."

He took a deep breath and looked out his window.

"You can pay me back with a quiet drive."

She backed up the car and turned down the street.

"I don't know," she said. "Twelve hours is a long time to be quiet."

He leaned his seat back and closed his eyes.

"Don't worry. After the first 11 hours, it will seem like a cakewalk."

She shook her head and looked down the road, as dawn's rosy fingers touched the edge of the world, where another teaspoon dipped into the ocean, and the night gave way to the budding dawn.

The End

Also available at Amazon:
THE BUTCHER'S WIFE
(A Special Jimmy Hunter Mystery Thriller)

A serial killer is terrorizing the city's streets, and Jimmy Hunter gets swept up in a sinister manhunt that will lead to terrifying twists and shocking discoveries even he can't handle.

Read on for a free preview …

BUT FIRST! Join my VIP Reader's Club.

You'll get exclusive promotions, complimentary goodies and other special surprises.
Visit www.rjlawbooks.com to join for free — I hope to see you there!

THE
BUTCHER'S WIFE
(A Jimmy Hunter Mystery Thriller)

By RJ Law

Chapter 1

Carol spread out a blanket and sat amid the spring grass, a fresh breeze tickling her bare arms as they warmed beneath the comforting sun. To her left, the river gurgled against the rocky shoreline, a trickling murmur like something from a dream.

She closed her eyes and filled her lungs, a magical scent dancing on the air. It was a faint hint of sweetness she couldn't quite place. Perhaps the smell of new honeysuckle in the offing? Or was it some colorful little ground flowers budding somewhere unseen? She didn't know and it didn't matter. Nothing mattered now but the easy smile on her face.

"Carol!"

She popped one eye open and saw her husband wrestling with his fishing pole.

"I got one!"

"Good for you, hon," she said as she closed her eyes and returned to her waking dream.

"Damn it!" he yelled. "I lost it."

Carol kept her eyes shut, her breathing deep and slow, senses alive, embracing everything.

"I can't fucking believe that," her husband said. "Brand new fucking line and it breaks on the fifth cast."

Carol's eyelids snapped open.

"Do you mind? I'm trying to meditate."

Her husband looked at her and frowned.

"How many sandwiches did you bring?"

Carol gestured toward the basket.

"Look for yourself and leave me be."

He threw down his pole and stomped over.

"Fucking 20-dollar line," he muttered as he bent over.

Carol sighed and shook her head, her pulse rate ticking up despite her practiced patience.

"Bologna?" her husband whined. "That's all you brought?"

Carol's eyes shot open again and she climbed to her feet.

"And what did you bring, Robert?"

Robert put his hands on his hips and started to say something but stopped when he saw the old man watching them from the road.

"Can I help you with something?" he asked with some heat in his words.

The old man gestured upriver.

"That your dog over there?"

Carol looked all around, but Buddy wasn't there.

"Shit," she muttered.

Robert scratched his head.

"Is it a Shephard?"

The old man nodded.

"Yessir," he said. "He don't look too friendly neither."

Carol frowned.

"He's very friendly," she said.

The old man bent over and spat.

"Not to my eye."

Robert shook his head.

"I'll go get him."

He stomped off and Carol followed, the old man watching with a sour look on his weathered face.

There were prickles in the grass, and they jabbed at her bare feet as she trotted up behind her husband, little curses leaking from between her lips with every step.

"Why weren't you watching him?" asked Robert as he stormed up the river.

Carol began a wicked retort, but it faltered when she heard the scream.

145

They stopped and listened, each looking at the other through wide, uncertain eyes. The wind licked the leaves and grasshoppers buzzed in the breeze.

Another scream.

"What the hell?" said Robert as he broke into a run.

"Robert!" cried Carol as she hurried behind him. "Wait!"

Robert ran through a patch of woods and popped out along the shoreline, where a small group of people had gathered at the water's edge. He slowed and approached, his eyes straining to see around them, heart throbbing within his chest.

"What's he got?" asked a fat woman with a green visor.

Robert pushed through them and looked downriver, where a German Shepherd pawed at the wet bank.

"Buddy!" Carol yelled as she caught up to him.

The dog continued its work, his head low, back turned.

"Buddy!" yelled Robert.

The dog turned and ran a few steps toward them, his face marred with blood and gore.

"Oh my God," said Carol.

Robert took a step toward the dog, and it growled.

"Buddy!" he yelled again, but there was a catch in his voice.

He took another step toward the dog, and it turned back toward the river, racing back to its original place where it appeared to be guarding a prize.

Robert approached and the little crowd followed, all of their faces painted with a medley of wonder and deep concern.

As they approached, the dog began growling again, his eyes fully dilated, mind possessed by feral thoughts.

"Oh my God!" cried the woman with the visor. "Is that a foot?"

Carol screamed and Robert clutched his stomach while Buddy laid down and gnawed at a toe.

Chapter 2

Jimmy sat behind the wheel of his car, eyes trained on the comings and goings at the nightclub across the street. There was a long line now, and the bouncer was turning people away. Lots of guys shook their heads in frustration as the big man moved all the scantily clad girls ahead and inside.

"Hey," the rejects yelled. "Come on. Give us a fucking break."

The bouncer looked at them and shrugged, a "what-do-you-expect" look on his face while all the pretty girls rushed inside.

"You, you and you," said the bouncer, his shoulders thrown back, a little snarl on his lips.

Jimmy looked the man over from afar. He had a bushy black beard and wore sunglasses at night. He stood probably six-foot-four, and his biceps were oiled. Jimmy squinted. Big, yes, but strong? Hard to say. More fat than muscle? Maybe, maybe not. Jimmy couldn't really tell from this distance anymore.

He squinted harder as he watched each gorgeous girl rush inside, the routine winners of the great genetic lottery that is life. Each one absolutely beautiful. Every bit special in her own little way.

For now, Jimmy thought as he spat out the window onto the street. Give them ten more years and we'll see.

Someone approached his car door, but he kept staring at the bouncer.

"Hey doll," said a craggy voice.

"Move along," said Jimmy, his eyes peering through the neon-lit night.

The hooker leaned over and propped her arm against his open window.

"What's the matter?" she asked. "You don't like gettin head?"

Jimmy pulled away from the stink of her mouth.

"I appreciate the offer," he said dryly. "But no thanks."

The woman stood back and spat on the pavement.

"Whatever," she said. "I don't want your old ass dick in my mouth anyways."

Jimmy watched her stumble away with a drug-addled gait. He sighed through his nose and squinted at the bouncer.

"Well," he said to himself as he opened his car door.

He stepped outside into the night and stood, a creak in his spine as he straightened his back. He grunted and rubbed at the fire in his hip. That young doctor said he'd need a replacement sooner rather than later. But at some point, it's like putting new tires on a broken-down Chevy, at least in Jimmy's mind.

He grunted a little and shifted his weight until his footing felt right. Then he took out his gun and closed the car door.

He slid the piece into his rear waistband beneath his jacket, the cold of the steel stinging his sweaty skin. As he trotted across the street, the organized crowd grew restless, each frowning in turn as he approached the front of the line.

"Hey," said a young man with slick curly hair. "Where the fuck do you think you're going? The line starts back there."

Jimmy kept walking.

"Hey," said the man as he stepped forward.

Without stopping, Jimmy palmed his face and pushed him backward.

"What the hell?" shouted one of the others as the curly-headed man fell backward against the sidewalk.

The bouncer watched all this with mute indifference, his true feelings concealed behind his ridiculous nighttime sunglasses and tangles of facial hair.

"What's your deal, pops?" he asked as Jimmy approached.

Jimmy slowed and looked up at the man who now seemed to loom twice as large in the clarity of the moment.

"Move aside," said Jimmy. "I got business with Vincent."

The bouncer frowned.

"You got business with the boss, you don't come this way. Go around back and talk to his boys."

Jimmy sighed and scratched his forehead.

"It's a bit of a walk and I got this thing with my leg."

The bouncer chuckled.

"Alright, old man," he said as he put his hand on Jimmy's shoulder. "It's time to go."

The line of rejects had molded into a little mob during the interchange and now they gasped in horror as Jimmy broke the bouncer's arm with a swift and sudden motion.

"My arm!" screamed the big man as he tumbled to the ground.

Jimmy watched the man with a bored, disinterested expression, the only one he owned.

"Pardon me," he said as he stepped around his writhing body and entered the club.

Inside, it was all noise and flashing lights, people screaming at each other over the music, drinks sloshing in their hands. Jimmy stood at the entryway and took it all in. A tangle of young bodies throbbed atop a huge dance floor, while a potpourri of contrasting perfumes and musk colognes stabbed up into his nostrils.

Just steps away from where he stood, lightly clad servers flashed by, their breasts pushed together, false rabbit ears bouncing atop their heads. A drunk lurched backward from a pool table and one of the girls screeched to a stop, the beer on her tray tipping forward as she struggled to dodge him. She fumbled helplessly as the bottle flipped from its perch and tumbled to the ground.

"Fuck!" she yelped as the drunk turned to view the damage.

"Oh," he said. "I'm sorry—"

Before he could finish, a large man in a suit swept in from the shadows and dragged him away, while his drinking mates watched through startled eyes.

"Goddammit," said the girl as she bent over to retrieve the spilled bottle.

Jimmy watched her bend, the bottom of her skirt sliding up over her buttocks.

"Jimmy!" said a skinny man with hollow cheeks and red cocaine eyes.

He slapped Jimmy on the back and smiled.

"What's with all the action out front?" he said. "You know you ain't gotta do that shit. Just come through the back. We'll take you right in."

Jimmy grunted.

"Sure," he said as he looked the man up and down.

He wore an ill-fitting suit that looked to have been made when he was twenty pounds heavier, and the polyester fibers shone wetly under the red strobing lights.

"What do you need?" asked the man as he rubbed at the burn in his nose.

Jimmy frowned.

"I need to talk to Vincent."

The skinny man snorted a few times and smiled.

"Naw, you need to tell me what you need, and then I can decide if it's worth the boss's time."

Jimmy narrowed his eyes and the man's smile faltered.

"Where's Vincent?" he asked.

The skinny man flexed his jaw muscles and leaned in close.

"Listen, we're all paid up with Mario."

Jimmy shook his head.

"This ain't about that."

The man pulled back and nodded.

"Alright," he said. "Stay here a second."

He turned and disappeared into the mass of people gyrating beneath the smoky red lights. Moments later, he returned with another at his side, this man taller and much more well-fed.

"This way," said the skinny man.

He turned and forced his way through the crowd, Jimmy following, the large man trailing a few steps behind. They reached the other side of the club and trotted up a narrow set of stairs that led to a long balcony that overlooked the entire floor, a mass of arms and legs, of drinking, dancing bodies. There stood another large man, his eyes cast downward at the people below.

"Yeah?" he muttered without looking up.

"He's here to see the boss," said the skinny man.

The man raised a thumb over his shoulder at a black steel door behind him.

"Go ahead."

The skinny man approached the door and knocked a couple of times. Then he gave the doorknob a twist and Jimmy followed him inside.

Before them at a broad oak desk, sat a bald man in a pink dress shirt, the collar open, a tailored gray suit vest over his muscled chest. A pale white scar ran the length of one cheek and down into a neatly trimmed beard, where a few gray threads sprouted out between a thick forest of dark black bristles.

"Uh, boss?" started the skinny man, but Vincent shut him up with one raised finger.

"Gimme a second," he muttered as he looked over a stack of papers. His eyes squinted through a pair of cheap reading glasses that were much too small for his face.

They waited several minutes, the skinny man pulling at his collar, Jimmy looking bored as ever. At last, Vincent finished with his papers and peered up over his glasses.

"Ah," he said with a smile. "Jimmy."

He tore the glasses from his face and sat back in his chair.

"To what do I owe the pleasure?"

Jimmy looked at the skinny man.

"I'd prefer to speak alone if that's alright."

Vincent snapped his fingers.

"Out," he said.

The skinny man rubbed his nose and stepped back.

"Yes, sir."

He rushed out of the office and closed the door behind him.

"Now," said Vincent. "What are you doing here? You know we're all paid up?"

Jimmy nodded.

"This isn't about that."

Vincent scratched the scar on his cheek.

"Alright, then, what's it about?"

Jimmy cleared his throat and swallowed.

"I need a favor."

Vincent's eyes widened.

"A favor?" He chuckled. "Well now, ain't that some shit?"

He shook his head and leaned forward.

"What can I do for you, Jimmy?" he said with false concern.

Jimmy frowned.

"I need to find someone."

Vincent propped his forearms against his desk.

"Who exactly are we talking about?"

Jimmy reached into his pocket and withdrew a folded sheet of paper.

"Name's Miles Francesa."

He passed the paper over to Vincent, who eyed the black and white mugshot with a frown.

"You know him?" asked Jimmy.

Vincent tossed the paper down onto his desk.

"Maybe," he said. "What's this for?"

Jimmy shrugged.

"He's a bail jumper."

Vincent shook his head and laughed.

"You got to be fuckin kidding me," he said. "You're still doing this kind of small-time shit for that crooked attorney?"

Jimmy shrugged.

"Gotta make ends meet somehow."

Vincent's face hardened.

"What's the problem? Mario not paying you enough?"

"I didn't say that," said Jimmy.

"But if he were, you wouldn't have to be doing this pathetic side work, ain't that right? Or is it that you got debts? Maybe that's the problem."

Jimmy stared forward with his even expression.

"Don't worry about me," he said flatly.

Vincent leaned back in his chair and eyed Jimmy from head to toe.

"You know, you ought to come work for me. A man with your talents, old as you are. There's still time to make some real money."

Jimmy looked at him, his eyelids lazy, always heavy, always low.

"I appreciate the offer, but I'm all set."

Vincent's face soured.

"What, you're too good to work for me?" he asked. "You'll shake people down for Mario, but you won't take drug money, is that it?"

Jimmy sighed.

"I don't judge anybody for how they make a living," he said. "It just ain't for me. Now, do you know this guy or don't you?"

Vincent nodded.

"Of course, I know him. I know everybody."

"Well," said Jimmy. "Do you know where I can find him?"

Vincent sucked at his teeth.

"What's it worth to you Jimmy? You willing to owe me a favor for this?"

Jimmy shrugged.

"Something proportional," he said. "That's all."

Vincent smiled.

"That's all I'd expect."

He reached into a desk drawer and took out a pen.

"He's hiding out here." He flipped the paper over and jotted an address on the back. "He's been there a couple days."

Jimmy watched him write.

"He work for you or something?"

Vincent shook his head.

"Nah, I don't know him, but he's tight with one of my boys. Old friends, I guess. Came to him in a rough state, begging for cover. So, my guy put him up in his basement."

He passed the paper over to Jimmy.

"And what about your man?" he said. "He gonna give me trouble?"

Vincent shook his head.

"I'll give him a call and tell him to stand aside. He won't like it, but he'll damn well do it."

Vincent nodded.

"I appreciate it."

Vincent scratched his beard.

"Of course, Jimmy," he said. "With all the crazy shit going on, guys like us gotta stick together."

Jimmy grunted and turned toward the door.

"And Jimmy," said Vincent. "Keep your hands off my guys, ok? I got a reputation to uphold. I can't have you manhandling my boys."

Jimmy opened the door without speaking.

"Remember, Jimmy," said Vincent as Jimmy shut the door behind him. "Even guys like you ain't immune to accidents."

Hours later, Jimmy sat behind his steering wheel outside a rundown house on a potholed road. In this decaying part of town, a large stinking refinery loomed large, smokestacks seeding the sky with a billowing smog of noxious air.

He opened the car door and stepped out amid the sharp stench of burning petroleum. He slipped his pistol into his rear waistband and trotted across the street, the clap of his shoes drowned away by the faint sound of sirens and highway traffic.

He stepped onto the gravel driveway and made his way toward the structure, a one-story shithole with a peeling shingled roof. Six crumbling concrete steps led up to a cracked front porch, where fat roaches scuttled amid the low porch light.

Jimmy scaled the steps and banged on the front door, a slight give beneath his shoe as he crunched one of the roaches down.

Heavy boot steps slammed down inside, and the door swung open.

"Yeah?"

It was a big man in a dirty wife-beater, his arms latticed with tattoos. He stared hard at Jimmy through another set of red cocaine eyes.

"I'm looking for Miles," said Jimmy.

The man kept staring.

"You Vincent's guy?" Jimmy asked.

The man firmed his mouth.

"Maybe," he said.

Jimmy sighed.

"Well," he said. "Is he here or not?"

The man snorted and stepped back.

"Yeah, he's here."

Jimmy stepped through the entryway and looked around.

The living room was a filthy place adorned with lawn furniture and pizza boxes. There was a stink on the air, unwashed flesh and spoiling food, a urine-soaked bathroom, and what was that other thing? A hamster cage maybe? Who could guess? Who would want to?

Jimmy looked down at the floor, where more roaches scurried about.

"Nice place you have here."

"Eat me," said the man as he brushed past him.

Jimmy followed him inside and put his hands in his pockets, the noxious refinery smell a happy memory now.

"Miles!" yelled the man, his voice rattling a framed photo against its crooked nail.

The man fell into a soiled recliner and leaned backward, the footrest popping up with a sickly squeal. Jimmy pushed his bottom lip out and tapped a shoe.

"You want a beer or something?" asked the man.

Jimmy started to answer but stopped when Miles skulked into the room.

"You Jimmy?" he asked, his face pointed toward the ground.

He had a sick look in his eyes but not in a drug-addled way.

"I am," Jimmy said.

Miles nodded.

"I'm ready."

The other man sat up fast and Jimmy almost went for his gun.

"Fuck this," he said. "You tell him what you seen."

Miles snapped his head around.

"Shut up, Tony," he said.

Jimmy watched them both, his eyelids relaxed, pulse the same.

"Well," he said. "We best be getting on."

Tony jumped up from his seat.

"You don't even care what he's got to say?"

Jimmy looked from one to the other.

"Not particularly," he said with his flat, disinterested voice.

He turned toward the door while Miles and Tony said their goodbyes.

Outside, huge flames danced atop the refinery stacks, the towering fires flaring brightly as they burned off excess gas. Jimmy watched them through lazy eyes, his lungs taking in the noxious output, a growing nausea in his gut.

"Hurry up," he called.

Seconds later, Miles stood beside him.

"You ready?" Jimmy asked.

Miles nodded and they moved down the porch, pain firing through Jimmy's bad hip with every downward step. When they got to the car, he stopped and looked at the young man.

"You're not gonna give me any trouble, are you?"

Miles shook his head.

"No, sir," he said. "I know who you are."

Jimmy nodded.

"Alright then."

They opened their doors and got inside.

"Go ahead and put your seatbelt on," said Jimmy as he cranked the engine.

Miles put his seatbelt on and sat back in his seat.

About 30 minutes later, Jimmy pulled the car up in front of a big brick house with a for-sale sign on the lawn.

"What is this?" asked Miles. "I thought you were taking me to the cops."

Jimmy shook his head.

"No, you're gonna stay here tonight with a babysitter. Your lawyer will make arrangements with the cops tomorrow."

Miles looked confused.

"Why?"

Jimmy shrugged.

"I'm not a lawyer," he said. "From what I understand, though, it's better this way. You stay here tonight. Let your attorney arrange your surrender. Might be able to swing something in your favor that way. I wouldn't count on it though."

Miles nodded.

"Fair enough."

He reached for the door handle.

"Hey," said Jimmy. "Let me ask you something. If you don't mind."

Miles shrugged.

"Alright."

Jimmy scratched his jaw.

"Who do you work for exactly? I mean, the shit they arrested you for, that ain't all you. No offense, but somebody big is behind it."

Miles looked at his lap and shook his head.

"You wouldn't know them."

Jimmy pinched his eyebrows together.

"I know everyone in this city," he said. "Everyone worth knowing anyway."

Miles looked at him, a strange glint in his eyes, almost like pity.

"Not them," he said.

Jimmy thought about that for a moment.

"How do you know I don't?"

Miles shrugged.

"Because if you knew who they were, you'd either be working for them, or you wouldn't be alive."

He wrenched the door open and stepped out of the car.

"Thanks for the ride," he said.

The young man shut the door and walked toward the brick house, where a big black man stood waiting in front of the open front door.

"Anytime," muttered Jimmy though Miles was much too far to hear.

An hour later, Jimmy pulled up to his place, a nothing little house he rented from an old lady with glaucoma in one eye. He parked his car in the driveway and got out, rubbing his leg and cursing his age. He unlocked the door and stepped inside, no movement or sound, just quiet throughout.

"Barney," he called out into the darkness.

A slow shuffling broke the quiet and a yellow retriever crept into the room, his old face weakly lit by the pale moonlight filtering through the window shade. Jimmy flipped on the kitchen light and the dog limped forward.

"Hey," whispered Jimmy as he knelt. "Come here."

The dog came closer, and Jimmy rubbed his ear.

"You hungry?"

He shut the door behind him and walked across the room. He opened the pantry and took out a large can of dog food. He worked it open with an old-school handheld can opener and shook the stubborn contents out with a wet shloomp into an empty metal bowl. The dog sniffed the food and ate. Jimmy scratched the dog's ear and opened the refrigerator door.

He made a bologna sandwich and tossed potato chips onto his plate. Then he went into the little living room and sat in his old, tattered recliner. He grabbed the remote and flipped on the television, the newsman prattling on about the economy and political polls, gas prices and whatnot.

"... and economists expect the consumer price index to increase in the short term with the recent events abroad," said a handsome man with a clean haircut.

Jimmy bit into his sandwich and chewed.

"And in local news," said a perky young woman with blinding-white teeth, "more human remains were recovered in the East River this evening, as police continue to investigate an alarming string of related killings."

"That's right, Kim," said the handsome man, a dazzling gleam in his deep blue eyes. "Police are investigating what may, in fact, be an apparent set of serial murders. To date, there have been at least a dozen victims, all identified only by partial remains."

Jimmy chewed and swallowed.

"But what does it all mean?" the newsman continued. "Is a serial killer at large in the greater metropolitan area? Doug Mathews is on the scene."

Jimmy bit into his sandwich again and chewed slowly as the camera panned the river, its dark water giving back the moonlight amid the ink-black night.

"A foot, a hand, a dozen more of the same," said Doug Mathews with his deep broadcaster voice. "These are the ghoulish treasures of a morbid exposition into the murky depths of the East River."

"Get back!" yelled a policeman at a line of frenzied reporters.

"What began as a tragic mystery has evolved into an ongoing crisis. Police have more questions than answers, but they do know one thing: This isn't normal."

"About ten bodies a year," said a broad-chested man in a decorated police uniform. "That's what we usually pull from the river on average."

"Ten bodies," said Doug Mathews. "A startling number. Tragic, disturbing, and yet paltry compared to what's happened in the past six months."

"Based on what we've seen," said the police chief, "we're investigating the possibility of a serial offender."

Jimmy turned as Barney nudged against his arm.

"Alright," he muttered.

He fingered loose a piece of bologna and passed it over. As the dog chewed, the TV kept screaming.

"But why only feet and hands?" asked Doug Mathews. "Where are the heads? Where are the torsos?"

Jimmy changed the station and rubbed Barney's head.

"It's a sick fucking world," he said to the dog as it whined for more bologna.

He tore off another slice and passed it over, while Andy Griffith grinned amid the black-and-white reruns of a simpler time.

The story continues in:

THE BUTCHER'S WIFE
(A Jimmy Hunter Mystery Thriller)

Available at Amazon!

Made in the USA
Las Vegas, NV
23 October 2024

10395296R10089